LOST PROPERTY

TRIALS & TRIBULATIONS OF
A PROVINCIAL ESTATE AGENT

by Jason Whichelow

BRITISH LIBRARY CATALOGUING-IN-PUBLICATION DATA. A catalogue record for this book is available from the British Library.

Published in Great Britain in 1995 by
Northumberland Publishing
30, Bury Road, Brandon, Suffolk, IP27 0BU

Cover cartoon by Sue King

ISBN 0 9526863 0 9

Printed and bound in Great Britain by
The Lavenham Press Ltd., Water Street, Lavenham, Sudbury, Suffolk, CO10 9RN

This book is dedicated to the memory of

Aimee

*A free spirit who brought fun and laughter
to the lives of many*

Estate agents develop a strange affliction known as Misleading Adjectives Deficiency (MAD) since abandoning their use of flowery language.

A typical small town agent becomes entangled in ever increasing misunderstandings, with hilarious results. Frank Lee suspects that MAD is caused indirectly by 'The Taxpayers' Money Mountain. Frank constantly clashes with his Regional Director, L. C., whom he refers to as 'Elsie' or 'El Cid'.

The reader meets the new 'pottily correct' Landpersons of the local pub, a demented electronic spellchecker, the odious firm of Floggitt & Quick and house buyers and sellers of varying eccentricity before a cure is found.

Lost Property dispels the myth that estate agents are 'all the same' and will appeal not only to those involved in the property industry but also to anyone who has ever wondered what estate agents actually do with their time.

~~~~~~~~~~~~~~

Acknowledgments

~~~~~~~~~~~~~~

December is always a quiet month in the property market and 1993 was no different in that respect. Out of boredom, I wrote what I hoped would be an amusing article and sent it off to 'The Estate Agent,' the journal of the National Association of Estate Agents. The editor, Peter Cliff and his assistant, Sally Whitehead, seemed to like it and included it in the February 1994 edition for which I was grateful.

Since everyone is supposed to have a book inside them, I wondered whether I would be able to produce one and continued scribbling at odd moments for the rest of that year and the spring of '95. This is the result.

I am also most grateful for the help and practical advice given to me by Eddie Stewart of Stewart Creative Services, Jenny Ahern, Chas Adams, Adrian Pugh and to Mandy Willimott who typed much of the manuscript.

~~~~~~~~~~~~~~

CONTENTS

CHAPTER I

Twigs in the Rain Forest

Standing in the newsagent's shop one morning, a headline caught my eye. 'FREDDIE HAMSTER ATE MY STAR' was printed bold on the front page of the 'The Stun.' Intrigued, I read the article beneath; apparently, a reporter's pet rodent had devoured an entire copy of a rival newspaper. Fascinating, I thought, but hardly earth-shattering news. My favourite daily paper had not been delivered at home that morning for some inexplicable reason, and I stood in a queue of other disgruntled customers waiting for a replacement.

We have a love-hate relationship with newspapers in my house. I love reading them and my wife hates me doing it when there's grass to be cut and redecorating to be done. The wallpaper's looked perfectly all right to me for the past 10 years; why it suddenly needs replacing on a Sunday morning is beyond my understanding! I would much rather be looking through the 'Mole on Sunday' and uttering the occasional snort of derision at the latest piece of nonsense from the politically correct brigade.

I believe we have America's First Lady to thank for helping to promote political correctness. Now, I have nothing against Americans; far from it. They have many admirable qualities but I just wish this particular peculiarity of the 1990s had stayed on the other side of the Atlantic. With any luck, it's just a passing fad and perhaps sanity will return in good time for the New Millennium.

Come to think of it, anyone who can name their daughter

'Chelsea' is probably capable of almost anything. I just hope Chelsea marries someone with a sensible surname, and not someone called Bunn or Pensioner or something. I can just imagine the scene in a sumptuous ballroom at Buckingham Palace. A flunky is announcing the honoured guests. 'Sir Percival Smooth-Twytte...... and the Hon. Miss Arabella Tartt.......' '....... Mr. Hiram T. Flowershow Jr...... and Mrs. Chelsea Flowershow.'

What would the Clintons have called Chelsea if she had been a boy, I wondered. 'Millwall,' possibly, or perhaps they would be relaxing in the White House one day discussing a forthcoming happy event and suddenly Hillary would turn to Bill and say something like 'Say, Honey, Queens Park Rangers Clinton sounds kinda cute!'

I glanced at my watch; only ten minutes to go before I had to open up my Estate Agents office just along the High Street. That's one of the advantages of running a business in a small Suffolk Town. No tiresome commuting by road or rail; the wrong type of snow or unexpected wet autumn leaves on the line hold no fears for me. I could still be on time if the people in front of me would just get a move on!

As I was waiting, I was irritated to overhear the manager tell a customer that he had just given out the last copy of my regular paper. Becoming increasingly impatient, I carried on browsing through the other newspapers on display. One of the broadsheets had a short report on the front page concerning the Housing Market. It quoted the Chief Executive of Far & Wide Building Society as saying that prices had increased the previous month by 0.95 per cent. The paper next to it carried a headline saying 'HOUSING SLUMP', followed by a brief statement attributed to the Chief Executive of Yookay Building Society to the effect that house prices had fallen by 1.25 per cent in the same period.

After that, I turned my attention from the 'heavies' to the tabloids. During the next few minutes, I learnt that an actor from 'Neighbours' is distantly related to the Royal Family and is 981st in line for the throne, Elvis Presley had been spotted cleaning windows at a supermarket in Norwich and that the Loch Ness Monster is gay. I wondered what was wrong with the provincial journalists on my regular paper. Why didn't they ferret out these interesting stories instead of concentrating on war, famine and the price of pig-feed?

A smaller headline at the bottom of a page came to my notice. 'ESTATE AGENTS MUST NOW STOP TELLING LIES,' it read. 'Hmmm,' I thought. Is this a classic case of the pot calling the kettle non-Caucasian, or what? I was about to read on when I became aware of a tapping noise, and realised with a start that I was the only customer left in the shop. I had been so engrossed that I had failed to notice that everyone else had gone. The newsagent stopped drumming his fingers on the counter.

'Would you like to borrow a few newspapers and return them later when you've read them?' he enquired with heavy sarcasm.

'That won't be necessary, my good man,' I retorted. 'Since you appear to have sold out of "The Beano" this will have to do instead!'

I settled up the weekly bill and quickly left the shop. I shoved the paper under my jacket with the all the furtive embarrassment of a teenager purchasing his first 'girlie' magazine. I hurried along to the office, said 'Good morning.' to the staff, shut myself in my private room and opened the paper.

I was immediately confronted by a three quarter page photograph of a scantily dressed lady baring her teeth and more-than-ample bosom at the camera. The caption informed me that this was Lusty Linda from Luton and that her ambitions were to travel, appear in 'Baywatch' and buy a house for her Mum. I hurriedly thumbed through the other pages which seemed mainly concerned with sport, t.v programmes, gossip about the Royal Family and horoscopes.

Finally, I came to the bit I was looking for. As I had

anticipated, the article headed 'ESTATE AGENTS MUST NOW STOP TELLING LIES' concerned the Property Misdescriptions Act which was about to come into force. The report was heavily biased and gave the impression that, until now, all Estate Agents had taken a perverse pleasure in writing totally fictitious sales literature but would now no longer be allowed to 'get away with it.'

I sighed.

Now, I am not going to pretend that all Estate Agents are, and always have been, honest, upright citizens. There is a rogue element in every business and profession and no doubt there always will be. Estate Agency is no different in that respect but to tar everyone with the same brush is absolutely ridiculous. Why, if someone was to tell me that not all journalists, or even politicians, are completely beyond reproach I would not be surprised in the slightest.

I could not help wondering why the reporter had decided to launch such an unfair attack. Maybe he had good reason to do so through personal experience. Somehow, I doubted it. Judging from the rather immature phrasing of the article, it was likely that he had not yet set foot on the bottom rung of the Property ladder. Possibly he had covered the Lusty Linda assignment and had found that she had been less lusty towards him than he had hoped. That could explain his petulant outpourings. I just did not know.

Probably the most likely explanation was that, as a novice reporter, he had preconceived ideas about most things and had soon come to realise that certain groups of people are fair game for the vitriolic pen treatment and are to be treated with contempt. What hypocrisy!

I sat and stared at the newspaper for a few moments and felt rather sorry for it. It had probably started life as a twig in a Brazilian Rain Forest where it had been quietly minding its own business, enjoying the sunshine and admiring the occasional multi-coloured butterfly that happened to alight upon it.

Suddenly, without warning, its world had literally

collapsed, the tree beneath it having been chopped down and transported across the oceans. The twig had then found itself pulped and, through some complicated process, re-constituted into 24 pages of juvenile trivia.

I carefully rolled up the newspaper and, taking careful aim, tossed it into a wastepaper basket on the far side of the room. As I watched it flying though the air, I reflected that, at last, Lusty Linda's ambition to travel had been realised.

CHAPTER 2

A Difficult Act to Follow

I went through to the kitchen, collected a cup of coffee and took it back to my office. I sifted through the morning's post and picked out the items requiring me to dictate replies. One of the letters was from a London Solicitor asking whether any progress had been made in finding a buyer for a property known as 9, Mafeking Terrace. I felt inclined to reply:

'Dear Sirs,

No.

Yours faithfully,'

but thought I had better be a little more expansive in case any further business was forthcoming.

9, Mafeking Terrace was the bane of my life. I had first been asked to value it three years earlier when the occupant, an eccentric old lady, had been considering selling and moving into a bungalow. She had lived a very spartan lifestyle, clearly having a deep distrust of newfangled features such as inside plumbing and electricity. Hardly surprisingly, it appeared that she did not venture to the outside privy after dark and instead used a chamber pot under the bed. Unfortunately, she did not empty it in the morning, but went out and bought a new one from the antiques shop on the corner. I noticed about half a dozen, each filled to overflowing, before making my excuses and dashing down the stairs and out into the garden.

I politely declined instructions to sell the property since, firstly, I felt she must have been nearly ninety and the move would probably have killed her and, secondly, no buyer would thank me for showing them over. The solicitor had written to me six months later saying that the old lady was now living in a nursing home. They had therefore instructed me to place the property on the market; apparently, the old lady had said that she would only entrust the matter to me since I had been 'such a nice young man.' I had therefore used the enclosed set of keys to make another inspection.

The property was in a serious state of disrepair and certainly not fit for human habitation. I had gone back to the office and dictated a set of particulars which stated the facts and warned people to be careful of the rotting floorboards; it was likely that they would arrive back on the ground floor faster than they went up.

It has always been my policy, whenever possible, to accompany prospective buyers and over the next year or two must have spent a total of several hours there. We gradually reduced the price, but to no avail. During this time I first heard of the Property Misdescriptions Act but thought it didn't really apply to me. I did not make a habit of using flowery descriptions and did my best to avoid misleading people. After all, today's buyers are tomorrow's sellers and they are highly unlikely to come back to me if I've upset them in the first place.

As time went on, the Act received more prominence in the trade press and it seemed that I would have to take it a little more seriously. Anxious to avoid falling foul of the law, I attended a seminar in an hotel conference room, organised by the local branch of the National Association of Estate Agents.

The speaker was a Management consultant who was highly knowledgeable in the field of Estate Agency. He lectured at great length, warning us that in future we had to take the utmost care in what we did or said, verbally or in writing. Human error would not save us from appearing in court; ignorance would be no defence. The Management

Consultant concluded his talk by saying that until the Act came into force, no-one could say how it would be interpreted.

After the coffee break I strategically placed myself by the exit before the question and answer session which was to follow. Most questions were of the 'what if........?' variety. Each hypothesis seemed more bizarre that the last. For some unknown reason, there are always one or two people at seminars who have a burning desire to obtain answers to the most unlikely questions.

'What if I stake out a building plot and a mad dog comes along and pulls one of the posts out with his teeth and runs off with it? Will I be held responsible?'

'What if my particulars state that the outside of a house is decorated with "Sandtex", but the typist puts "Semtex" by mistake, and nobody notices until it is pointed out by someone on the mailing list? Could I be prosecuted?'

I decided that I would be more usefully employed propping up the bar next door and went off in search of liquid refreshment. It may have been my imagination but I thought the lecturer looked rather envious as I headed off towards the bar.

It all seemed to me to be a fuss about nothing. I went back to the office the following day and carried on as normal. Reports and opinions continued to appear in the trade press and I became increasingly uneasy. I had assumed that the purpose of the Property Misdescriptions Act was simply to curb the worst excesses of the minority rogue element and that everyone else would be left in peace. A somewhat näive view as it turns out!

I attended another seminar just before the Act came into force, this time with trading standards officers in attendance. It still appeared that no-one could say exactly what constituted an offence. A transgression would be recognised after it had happened, however, and prosecution would almost certainly follow. The following day, sitting at my desk, I gave consideration to what I should do next. Who would have thought it would be so difficult to avoid misleading people?! From the information that I had gathered over the past few months, it appeared that estate agents would no longer be able to say or write anything which was untrue.

No one running a reputable business could possibly argue with that. However, it was also confirmed that we could no longer rely on information given to us by another party e.g. the house owner, without first seeing documentary evidence. Furthermore, for the purposes of the Act, photographs, drawings, etc., and even facial expressions and body language of the Agency staff and myself, were to be deemed a 'statement.' I could see that life was going to become even more confusing than it was already!

I suddenly felt very vulnerable; one small typing error that went un-noticed or one act of carelessness by one of the staff or myself and I could find myself in court facing a hefty fine and a criminal record. As an independent agent it was my place to make sure I knew all about the new regulations and to ensure that nothing went wrong. That was one of the advantages the chains of estate agents run by financial institutions have over me; people who are employed to keep abreast of legislation and organise numerous meetings to help keep the sales staff from getting into trouble.

I then had a brilliant idea. I decided to ring my old friend, Frank Lee, to find out what precautions his firm was taking. I had known Frank for many years since we had once worked together for the same firm and had later started up our own estate agencies in different towns. We had then both sold our businesses to financial conglomerates when it had been fashionable to do so towards the end of the 1980s and continued running our respective offices. Frank had remained with the Building Society owned chain, whilst I had become a born-again independent two years later.

Although he was obliged to attend some meetings that we both regarded as a total waste of time and money, I had to admit that others had their uses. I should mention at this stage that Frank had some weird and wonderful views on many subjects and could be a bit of a bore.

'What do you think of this Property Misdescriptions Act?' was my opening gambit.

'Well, I don't really see the point of it,' he said. 'As I understand it, very few official complaints were made about estate agents on the grounds of misdescription in the past. We've all seen magazine articles featuring examples of outrageous sales literature, but I'm inclined to think that most of them were the efforts of some Fleet Street hack with a fertile imagination and a deadline to beat.'

He paused for breath and I quickly interrupted to steer him away from one of his favourite hobby-horses, otherwise he would have carried on in the same vein for half an hour.

'Surely if it curbs some of the activities of the cowboy element it can't be a bad thing?' I suggested. 'What I want to know is, how can I avoid the pitfalls? Someone's bound to make a mistake sooner or later. We're all human, after all. Even the mob you work for!'

He ignored the jibe. I suspected he was somewhat envious of the fact that I was my own master again whereas he was halfway up the chain of command and there would always be someone applying pressure from above.

'The short answer is that you can't avoid making mistakes, no matter how careful you are,' he said. 'You'll just have to hope no-one notices when you do!'

'If the number of complaints in the past have been virtually non-existent, why did someone go to all this trouble?' I asked. 'What's the point in trying to control a problem that, to all intents and purposes, doesn't exist?'

'Ah, I've got a couple of theories about that,' he said. I was afraid that he would have, but I was curious to know what they might be and he was pleased to have the opportunity of airing them.

'Firstly, I believe the Government has come up with a new

way of tackling unemployment,' he told me.

'I'm not quite sure I follow,' I said.

'Well, it's obvious the trading standards department is undermanned at the moment. I believe that a new training scheme will be announced and by the end of the year there will be another three million officials enforcing compliance in various industries including the Property Market. Result: zero unemployment!'

I was impressed. Frank had a reputation for coming up with some daft theories, but this was exceptional even by his standards. Curiosity got the better of me and, in spite of myself, I had to ask what the other theory was.

'The Taxpayers' Money Mountain,' was the rather unexpected reply.

He rightly assumed from my baffled silence that I had no idea what he was talking about.

'Forget about Butter Mountains, Wine Lakes and the like, this is an all-British affair. I suspect that a clerical error in the last Budget resulted in everyone being charged more tax than was intended, hence an embarrassing surplus of cash in the Government's coffers!'

I could feel a headache coming on. I was never quite sure whether he was joking, or whether he really was stupid.

'What has that got to do with anything?' I asked.

He explained patiently, in the manner one would use when dealing with an especially dense five year old.

'Since no-one wants to admit that a mistake has been made, emergency measures have been introduced to eliminate the Taxpayers' Money Mountain before anyone, especially the Press, realises it exists.'

He paused for dramatic effect before playing his trump card.

'Someone has therefore come up with the brilliant idea of the Property Misdescriptions Act.'

'I'm afraid you've lost me,' I told him.

He sighed audibly down the telephone.

'The cost of all those extra officials, in terms of salary alone, not to mention the time and money involved at magistrate's courts, is going to be colossal. The surplus should be reduced in no time, making the Taxpayers' Money Mountain a thing of the past.'

I could think of no good reason for carrying on the conversation and thanked him for his time. I was obviously going to have to cope with these problems on my own. I decided I had no choice but to go through every set of particulars on my registers with a fine tooth comb and remove adjectives and personal opinions. Since 9, Mafeking Terrace was the cheapest property on my books, I started with that; not many adjectives to remove there! I looked at the final paragraph and realised that my attempts to be helpful would no longer be acceptable.

> 'N.B. Although the property requires a considerable amount of expenditure, as previously mentioned, this has been reflected in the asking price. The house stands in a pleasant residential area within easy walking distance of the town centre and, with sympathetic renovation, could be made into a most attractive and charming home.'

I felt the first sentence was fairly safe. The next one raised a number of questions.

'A pleasant residential area' was a widely accepted opinion locally but it was possible that not everyone would agree. That would therefore have to come out.

'Within easy walking distance of the town centre.' Obviously not as far as the 90 year old previous occupant had been concerned; therefore that would have to be deleted.

'A most attractive and charming home'; only if that was the type of property someone wanted. If a family was looking for a brand new house on an estate, they would find this property neither attractive nor charming.

In the end, I simply deleted the whole paragraph; people

would just have to look at the place and make up their own minds about the possibilities.

After I had finished changing the particulars of all the properties on my books, they were re-typed and printed. The job took two weeks as we fitted it in at odd moments whilst trying to carry on our normal business. I then sent a copy of the new particulars to each individual house owner, explaining why it had been thought necessary to change the sales literature concerning their property. Where appropriate, I asked for proof that they had had electric re-wiring or re-plumbing carried out, confirmation that the central heating was in working condition, photocopies of double glazing and cavity wall insulation guarantees etc, etc.

In order to avoid any misunderstanding and to pacify any irate house sellers in advance, I explained that I was simply trying to comply with the new Act. I went on to say that, personally, I did not doubt that what they had previously told me had been true.

It was difficult to see who was going to benefit from this new Act. Most vendors are proud of their homes and like the sales particulars to reflect their hard work and expenditure on improvements. House buyers would no longer find it easy to differentiate between particulars of several properties with similar accommodation. This would make it more difficult for them to weed them out before going to view. It also seemed likely that trading standards officers, magistrates and others would spend countless hours in dealing with cases where no loss had been suffered by any party whatsoever. I felt sure that they had far more important things to do.

Estate agency was certainly entering a new era and, like it or not, we were all going to have to get used to it.

CHAPTER 3

Less Than Total Recall

Unfortunately, I am not blessed with a very good memory and that does lead to some embarrassing situations in my business. Salesmen of 'Memory Courses' will no doubt say that everyone has the ability to improve their recollection of people and events with the benefit of correct training, and I am sure they are right. The problem is, trying to muster the perseverance to deal with the matter.

I was sitting at home one Sunday with the family enjoying a peaceful afternoon away from the telephone, reading the newspapers as usual. There was a small piece in one of them quoting statistics supplied by the Yookay Building Society; apparently, prices had increased on average by 2.65 per cent during the first six months of the year. The business section of my other paper informed me that prices had actually fallen during the same period by 1.95% per cent. They acknowledged Far & Wide Building Society's help in supplying these figures to them.

Suddenly, an advertisement at the bottom of the page caught my eye. The advert featured a photograph of a bespectacled man with a domed forehead peering intently out of the page at me. This, I was informed, was Professor Ernest 'Memory' Laine, who had mastered the technique of acquiring a prodigious memory. He could now memorise fifty two packs of playing cards and recall the exact sequence, backwards or forwards. He was able to glance through a telephone directory and instantly provide any telephone number requested.

'Just what I need!!' I said.

I read aloud from the advertisement, "Astound your friends, amaze your colleagues, the best investment you'll ever make......." It only costs £99.99 and worth every penny,' I went on.

My wife looked puzzled.

'Wouldn't it be cheaper to ring up Directory Enquires?' she asked.

'No, no,' I said. 'It's not telephone numbers I need to remember, it's people's names. It's most important that I train myself to put names to faces. This guarantees results. Money back if not delighted. I'll send off for it first thing tomorrow morning.'

'But I thought you'd done that a couple of weeks ago,' she said.

'Nonsense,' I said 'I've never seen this advert before.'

'Yes, you have,' she said. 'Don't you remember, you said then that Professor "Memory" Laine would make all the difference to your business life and that never again would you forget anyone's name, even if you met them twenty years later. You said you'd send off for it straight away. You must have forgotten about it.'

'That's ridiculous!' I said. 'Of course I haven't forgotten. How can I forget something I didn't know about in the first place?'

The argument continued along these lines for fifteen minutes, with neither of us giving way. I cut the coupon out of the advert, filled in my name and address and put it in an envelope ready to be posted when I got to the office the next day.

The following morning, I was in the bathroom when I heard the doorbell ring and my wife went to answer it. Two minutes later, she came in with a parcel.

'The postman just delivered this,' she said smugly. 'It's your memory course.'

It was a moment or two before I remembered what she was talking about. I quickly recovered my composure.

'That's amazing,' I said. 'They've delivered it already and the coupon is still in my jacket pocket. That's what I call service!'

I hurried out of the bathroom, ducking to avoid the wet flannel whistling past my right ear. I decided it would be prudent to go straight to the office and wait until the evening before examining the contents of the parcel.

Arriving at the office, I stopped to have a few words with our receptionist, Cindy. Now, buying and selling houses is an important transaction in anyone's life and consequently the agent is expected to recognise every caller instantly. He is also expected to be able to recall every minute detail of the negotiations without the need to consult the files.

Cindy had therefore been instructed to always ensure that I knew exactly who every caller was before ushering them through to my office. I was therefore caught on the hop when the front door burst open.

A burly man in his mid 30's with a ruddy complexion marched straight over to me. He was prematurely bald, apart from some straggly bits of hair at the back of his head tied into a pigtail with a rubber band. He had an irritating habit of turning every sentence into a question, mostly by adding the word 'Yeah.' We took an instant dislike to one another. He shoved his face belligerently close to mine and poked his finger at my chest. I was rather surprised that he was able to lift his hand, since it was considerably weighed down by a large ring on each finger and a chunky gold bracelet dangling from his wrist like a manacle.

'You're in charge here, yeah?' he demanded.

I nodded.

'My house, yeah?'

He paused expectantly.

I again nodded, signifying that I had managed to follow the conversation thus far.

'You're still trying to sell it, yeah?'

Desperately trying to remember who he was, I felt it safe to reply in the affirmative. I certainly didn't want to lose face by admitting I didn't know what he was talking about.

'No-one's been to view it for three weeks, right?'

There was another pregnant pause. I hesitated.

'Er, would you excuse me for just one moment?' I asked.

I scribbled out a note and handed it to my receptionist.

'Deal with that as quickly as you can, would you, Cindy?'

Surreptitiously she read the note, which said, 'Who the hell is he?'

She wrote on it and handed it back. I glanced at it.

'Haven't a clue,' it said.

'Great!' I thought. Still not wanting to admit my ignorance, I tried a different approach to try and jog my errant memory.

'Maybe the price is at fault,' I mused. 'What are we asking at the moment?'

He looked exasperated and raised his eyes to heaven.

'We,' he mimicked sneeringly, 'We, are asking £99,999. I wanted to ask a hundred grand but your Lister, yeah? Your Lister, right, said it would sound better at £99,999.'

By now, I was even more confused. As a small independent agent inspecting every property personally, I had no need for a Lister. I realised that further floundering on my part was pointless and decided to admit that I was completely baffled. Before I could do so however, he continued his ranting.

'I'm just about fed up with you lot,' he bellowed. 'You haven't sold my house, you don't know the price and you don't even know who I am. I'm taking the house off your books, right this minute, and giving it to that little firm across the road. Get my meaning?'

Suddenly, everything became abundantly clear to me. I told him that I most certainly had got his meaning but that he appeared to be in the wrong premises. For the first time since entering the office, the caller seemed unsure of himself. He hesitated and looked around at his surroundings, as if for the first time.

'Isn't this Floggitt & Quick Property Services?' he

demanded.

Without a word, I grasped his elbow and steered him over to the window. Silently, I indicated the office on the other side of the street. It had the name of the firm emblazoned across the front in neon lettering and the windows were lit up like a Mississippi Showboat. Difficult to miss it, I would have thought. The front door opened as we watched. If a dixieland jazz band had come marching out, I would not have been surprised in the least. However, it was just Daryl the lister scuttling off on an appointment, little white socks twinkling in the sunlight.

'I think you need to be over there,' I said. 'We're the Little Firm Across the Road.'

He strode out slamming the door behind him and muttering 'You could have said so before, right?'

'Best of luck!' I thought, as I watched him march across the road to see my despised opposite neighbours.

I found Floggitt & Quick to be a regular pain in the neck, to mention but one part of the anatomy. They were the type of firm who gave Estate Agents everywhere a bad name. No trick was too low for them to contemplate, provided there was a possibility of money involved. Since there is no restriction at present, anyone can open an Estate Agents office and they frequently do.

Gavin Floggitt had been in the antique furniture manufacturing business, specialising in producing items such as Tudor coffee tables which, he assured his gullible clientele, were absolutely genuine. His friend, Daryl, had been through several sales-related jobs including selling replacement windows, garage doors and foam-filled cavity wall insulation; it therefore seemed a logical step to start selling complete houses.

Daryl's big chance came when Gavin's Granny had died leaving her sweet shop in the High Street to him. They immediately decided to go into partnership as Estate Agents and opened up at the earliest possible moment. They started by getting Gavin's Aunt Mabel's name and address on the mailing list of every agent in town. As soon as property particulars dropped onto her doormat, Daryl would pay each property a visit and try to persuade the owners to put their houses onto his registers.

They also knocked on doors of houses where other agents boards were displayed outside. Not having any genuine buyers yet, they invented names of people who would 'definitely' buy. Relying on the fact that several owners were anxious to sell and were therefore much more susceptible, they telephoned them day and night until they finally gave in and agreed to 'sack' their original agents and deal with Floggitt and Quick instead.

They scoured the obituary columns in the local newspapers and rang the recently bereaved, offering their condolences along with their services, should a house need to be sold. If anyone complained that no prospective purchaser had been to view, someone was sent along within half an hour or so. This was frequently Gavin's wife, Daryl's girlfriend, the office cleaning lady or one of their mates from the pub, each posing as a bona fide buyer and promising to 'think about it.' This gave Gavin a bit of breathing space to find a genuine buyer before the owner took his business to another firm.

Another favourite trick was to gaze out of the office window and wait until they saw another agent's car pause at the traffic lights. (They knew every negotiator's car by sight). Daryl would then rush out and jump into his Ford Escort with the 'go faster' stripes along the sides which had been conveniently left parked on the yellow lines. He would then follow his quarry with all the cunning of a latter day James Bond, ensuring that his presence went unnoticed. As soon as the other agent arrived at his destination, Daryl would wait just around the corner until he had finished his business and driven away. Daryl would then go and knock on the door, introduce himself and offer to help sell the house.

This plan occasionally backfired when Daryl discovered

he was talking to the other negotiator's Mum, girlfriend or whatever but, having skin like a rhinoceros, he didn't let it worry him in the slightest. He was just happy that he managed to sign up the punters, as he referred to them, from time to time.

He remembered with glee the time he had gone into a house five minutes after the other negotiator had left. The owners had serious financial problems and required a quick sale although they could not afford to sell too cheaply. In the circumstances, since they were desperate, they allowed Daryl to handle the sale in addition to the other agent.

He had immediately returned to the car and contacted Gavin on the mobile phone, giving him details of the accommodation and price. He had then seen the other negotiator's car travelling in the opposite direction and continued trailing him for the rest of the afternoon. Daryl and his adversary had arrived back at their respective offices within two minutes of each other. It transpired that Gavin had managed to sell the house in the meantime at a knock-down price to a friend of his who had promised him a 'drink' out of it.

Gavin and Daryl had then congratulated themselves on their remarkable business acumen and opened a bottle of whisky in the office by way of celebration. It did not occur to them that the owner of the property had, through desperation, accepted far less for it than he should have done and would continue to suffer financially; it would not have bothered them if they had. The important thing was that they would receive a fee in due course.

Most Estate Agents would welcome some form of registration to keep out the 'Cowboy Element.' This would not only benefit the public who would know they were dealing with someone who is reliable and honest but also help the vast majority of agents who fall into this category. Perhaps something similar to a driving licence could be produced. Trainee Listers would have a provisional licence and be obliged to wear 'L-plates' around their necks whilst they accompanied experienced members of staff. After an initial training period of say, six months, they would be required to pass a test before being allowed to deal with something as important as someone's home.

Anyone wanting to set up business on their own account would have to apply for a provisional licence and work for another agent for two consecutive years before being let loose on the public. They would then obtain a 'full licence' to practice and, if any serious complaints were substantiated, their licences would be endorsed. Under a totting-up system they would face losing their licence if they were in the habit of committing serious misdemeanours. Maybe this system wouldn't be foolproof but it could rid the property world of the likes of Floggitt and Quick!

During my absence at the office, my wife had tidied the memory course away and put it in a safe place. It lay there forgotten for several weeks before I happened to come across it again.

CHAPTER 4

Questioners' Gardentime

People tend to have preconceived opinions of Estate Agents. It's hardly surprising since some sections of the media are either openly hostile or treat us as a joke. No doubt we are partly to blame for this situation. If we had demanded more control years ago we would, perhaps, have kept out the rogue element which some newspapers and television personalities seem to think typify the profession.

I well remember an incident which happened shortly after I left school in South London many years ago. I happened to bump into a school friend I had not seen for a few weeks. He had not been one of the star pupils of my class; in fact, he was rather dimwitted and slightly less academic than I was. When I told him that I was working as an office junior at an Estate Agents, a look of amazement came over his face and he said something like, 'What do you want to work for a bunch of crooks for?' This was accompanied by guffaws, hoots of derision and exaggerated thigh slapping.

His reaction rather surprised me, especially since the firm I was working for was one of the most prestigious in London, but I would not have expected him to have known that. I did wonder, however, how a sixteen year old, living in a property rented by his parents in Tooting, had been able to form an opinion on the subject. I am still waiting to be enlightened.

Maybe I'm easily offended but I'm inclined to be just as indignant about ignorance shown to my adoptive region as I am to my chosen career. Having lived more than half my life in East Anglia, I cringe whenever I hear actors attempting a Suffolk or Norfolk accent on television. They obviously haven't the faintest idea what one sounds like and have not bothered to take the trouble to find out.

Minor irritations even crop up on programmes like 'Question of Sport.' David Coleman is the chairman of this normally innocuous entertainment which comprises a quiz between two teams of sporting celebrities. Blackburn United footballer, Chris Sutton, once mentioned his former team-mates at Norwich City. For some inexplicable reason, Coleman felt compelled to adopt a 'Mummerset' accent and utter the immortal words 'Ooo-Arrr!' When I had finished laughing, I wondered what the man thought people did with their time in East Anglia. No doubt he assumed that everyone wore smocks, chewed straws and muttered 'Ooo-Arrr' while they harvested the sugar-beet!

One miserably wet Sunday afternoon, I turned on the radio just as someone was mentioning Estate Agents. Since the programme was 'Questioners' Gardentime,' I was a little surprised, to say the least and delayed switching over to something else.

'Does the panel think that Estate Agents should be made to put more detail about gardens in their publicity blurb?' asked the questioner.

One of the panellists, Fred Canker, gave his opinion.

'Yes, I think they should,' he replied. 'I believe it would be a great help to know the acid content of the soil.'

He then launched himself into the subject at great length and the rest of the panel agreed with him. I groaned. The Property Misdescriptions Act had only been in force for five minutes and now these people where jumping on the bandwagon. Wasn't life difficult enough?

I tried to imagine the consequences if the panellists got their way. Each negotiator would be issued with a soil-testing kit and a Readers Digest gardening book. 'Popular Gardening' magazine would be obligatory reading amongst

Listers. Bus loads of them would be shipped off on guided tours around Kew Gardens. Human error, however, would always appear, despite the efforts made by the management.

At a Magistrates court in Milton Keynes, a defendant is standing before the bench, looking sheepish. He states that his name is Darren and that he is employed as a Lister. The chairman, being unfamiliar with the word, assumes it to be some new-fangled term for Articled Clerk and decides to be facetious.

'And do you list to port or starb'd,' he enquires and is immediately overcome with mirth at his own ready wit.

Darren has no idea what he is talking about, smiles dutifully and says nothing. The Magistrate recovers his composure and gets down to business. Following a complaint concerning property particulars prepared by Darren, trading standards officers have investigated and decided to prosecute under the Property Misdescriptions Act. Apparently, a Mr. & Mrs. Bugg had done a three hundred mile round trip to view 'Dunroamin.' They were very annoyed to find that the 'immaculate lawns' were 95 per cent moss and the hybrid tea roses turned out to be floribunda.

'What have you to say for yourself, young man?' asks the Magistrate.

Unfortunately, Darren, not having yet been on the gardening course arranged by his employer wouldn't know a floribunda from a bucket of horse manure. He has a feeling that hybrid tea is the posh beverage that his Granny drinks and looks thoroughly bewildered by the whole proceedings.

'I didn't write them, did I?' he says.

'I'm asking the questions,' replies the Chairman, with a sigh. 'Are you, or are you not, responsible for this sales literature?'

'Yes, yer Honour, I mean no,' Darren replies. 'That is, I

mean they're on my paper but I didn't write them.'

The Magistrates are now all thoroughly confused and one of them demands an explanation. It transpires that Darren obtained another agent's particulars through some underhand method and contacted the owner, claiming to have a buyer. The owner had believed him, allowed him to offer the house for sale and Darren had had the particulars copied onto his own firm's paper, unbeknown to his employers, rather than taking the trouble to prepare his own.

The Magistrates are not impressed, fine him £500 plus costs and shortly afterwards he is seen walking towards the Job Centre, the management having relieved him of his car.

By this time, the Team had got onto another subject and I switched off the radio. It was still pouring with rain outside and I turned on the television, just in time to catch the tail-end of the News.

The newscaster was beaming at his unseen audience and saying, '....... and now, good news for homebuyers. The Yookay Building Society announced today that the recent drop in interest rates means that properties are now more affordable to young first time buyers.'

I was puzzled. Was my already shaky memory getting even worse? I searched around for the business section of one of the Sunday papers and found the bit I was looking for. Somebody described as a Property Market Analyst was giving his opinion that the recent reduction in interest rates would 'inevitably' lead to a surge in prices as buyers regained confidence in house purchase.

So, the 'good news' about interest rates was, after all, bad news for homebuyers. By now, I was totally confused, and I'm in the business. I wondered how the average first time buyer is supposed to make sense of these conflicting reports.

Perhaps we'd all be better off if these so-called experts kept their opinions to themselves. Either that, or they could consider talking to each other before making any pronouncements, coming to an agreement and then informing the media of their prophecy. We could all then sit back and watch as the opposite happens.

CHAPTER 5

Lost Property

Since we are in a part of Suffolk which contains two huge USAF bases, we frequently deal with American Personnel. Some of them live on base in military accommodation and I have heard that a few never venture beyond the perimeter fence during their tour of duty, which normally extends to three years or more. Many, however, prefer to live in the local community, making lasting friendships and renting or buying property in the area. This has certainly helped the local property market and many business people have bought properties solely for letting purposes, a few having made a fortune that way.

Some owners have temporarily moved elsewhere with jobs out of the area or abroad and have let their houses to USAF personnel whilst they are away. I have managed property on behalf of Landlords for many years and have found the vast majority of American tenants to be conscientious, usually paying the rent on time and keeping the property clean and tidy. There have, of course, been one or two exceptions despite all the efforts we make to ensure that everything runs smoothly for all concerned.

A few months ago, a client called in to say that he was going to work abroad for a while and would want to move back in eventually upon his return. He did not want to leave the property unoccupied during his absence and would obtain a useful income from letting it. He instructed us to handle the matter for him. Shortly after he left the Country we arranged a letting to a Texan sergeant and his family. The sergeant signed the Assured Shorthold tenancy agreement and checked the inventory and Statement of Condition which I had prepared. Everything was in order and he and his family proved to be exemplary tenants. The rent was always paid on the due date and the house was spic and span when I called to carry out the final inspection at the end of the tenancy. I carefully checked through the inventory and, since there were no damages, returned his deposit in full.

The landlord moved back into his house that evening, the tenant started a new tenancy on another property we were letting and everyone was happy, or so I thought.

The telephone was ringing when I opened the office next morning; it was the erstwhile landlord and he was hopping mad. He demanded to know what had happened to one of his rose bushes. Apparently, it had been of great sentimental value since it had been given to him and his wife on their Silver Wedding anniversary, had pride of place in the garden and was now nowhere to be seen. Since my inventory did not include every shrub in the garden, it had been omitted and I could not recall seeing it in the first place. I promised to investigate.

Perhaps I should mention at this stage that, no matter how careful Military tenants are with the house, few of them have the slightest idea of how to look after a garden, beyond mowing the lawn. I telephoned the USAF base, asked to speak to the former tenant and spent the next ten minutes being passed backwards and forwards through the switchboard to various departments before tracking him down. I wondered, not for the first time, what would have happened if I was ringing to report that World War III had broken out.

When I was eventually put through to the sergeant, I explained that I was trying to solve the mystery of the missing rosebush and it was apparent from the puzzled tone of his voice that he did not have the vaguest idea of what I was talking about. I tried a different tack. Had he tidied up the garden before he'd vacated the property? He became somewhat indignant.

'I sure did,' he replied. 'I cut the grass, swept the patio and even ripped out a God-damned cactus.'

I felt uneasy.

'This, um, God-damned cactus,' I asked. 'Did it have yellow flowers and thorns?'

'It sure as hell did,' he said. 'Spikes all over it - I ripped it out and threw it in the trash. Someone could've gotten hurt!'

I went white.

This was Suffolk not the Nevada Desert. Tenants were not supposed to do this sort of thing. Why couldn't he have just ignored the garden like everyone else did? I could see no point in pursuing the matter but asked him to contact me next time he saw a cactus, rattlesnake or anything else unusual in his garden before he did something drastic in future.

In the interests of pacifying the owner and maintaining good relations, I visited the local garden centre, bought a similar variety of rose bush, called round and presented it to him. Fortunately, he was somewhat mollified by my peace-offering and was able to see the funny side of the story. For my own part, I had learnt a useful lesson and took more interest in gardens of tenanted properties from then onwards.

When I got back, I found that Cindy had made a note in my diary for me to inspect and value a property on the edge of the town. Apparently, it was owned by a Mr. Bradshaw who had bought it through my firm five years previously. His wife had sadly died six months earlier and although he had persevered on his own for a while he now wanted to move down to Kent to be near his daughter and her family.

Mindful of the ever-vigilant Floggitt & Quick, I sauntered down the High Street and called in at the unisex hairdresser. Having made prior arrangements with the proprietor, I walked through the salon, out through the back door into the street behind and carried on into the public car-park. No doubt Gavin and Daryl were wondering why I had had my hair cut there three times that week.

I arrived at the property, which was a three bedroom bungalow similar to many favoured by couples retiring to the area from London and the Home Counties. I knocked on the door and Mr. Bradshaw let me in. Whilst I was sorry to learn why he was moving, it is always gratifying when people come back, whatever the reason.

I had a good look around the property, taking room measurements and making notes. This procedure was second nature and almost achieved by engaging automatic pilot. It was, that is, until The Property Misdescriptions Act had come into force. I was now taking copious notes and metaphorically walking on eggshells. We went into the lounge.

'That's 18' x 12',' Mr. Bradshaw informed me helpfully.

'I'm sure it is,' I said diplomatically, 'but I'd better just check to make certain.'

I took a reading on my new-fangled sonic measuring gadget.

'Actually, it's 17'11" x 11'11",' I said.

Mr Bradshaw flourished a set of particulars I had prepared five years earlier.

'Well, it must have shrunk then,' he said with a smile. 'You said it was 18' x 12' when we bought it.'

I quickly changed the subject.

'Have you carried out any alterations or changed the property materially in any way since you've been here?' I asked.

By this time, I had reached the bathroom, followed closely by Mr. Bradshaw.

'I had a new bathroom suite put in last year,' he informed me proudly. 'We weren't sure whether to have Dove Grey or Pampas but ended up with Ivory. It cost a lot of money.'

'Did you keep the receipt?' I asked.

'Well, no. I don't think so,' he replied.

'Sorry,' I said. 'I can't describe it as nearly new in my particulars unless I see the receipt. Neither can I mention the colour.'

He became slightly less friendly.

'Don't you believe me?' he asked. 'I bought it last year, I'm telling you. Anyway, you can put the colour in; you can see what colour it is for yourself.'

'It's not as easy as all that,' I told him. You've told me it's Ivory but it could be Champagne or Honeysuckle or some other fanciful label given to it by the manufacturers.'

He began to look rather irritable.

'Does it matter that much?' he asked.

'I'm afraid it does,' I said.

'We have to be so careful these days,' I explained patiently. 'This may sound a bit silly, but if we describe the bathroom suite in our particulars as "Ivory", people could mistakenly gain the impression that it's made out of elephants' tusks. They could then travel many miles to make an inspection and be disappointed when they find its made of fibreglass.'

He gave me an incredulous look.

'Why the devil would anyone want a bath made out of elephants' tusks?' he demanded. 'It would leak! Anyway, it was sold to me as Ivory.'

'Yes, but you can't prove it,' I said.

'Besides,' I added. 'Builders' Merchants are not bound by The Property Misdescriptions Act and I am.'

He was about to speak when I held up my hand to signify that I was giving the matter my undivided attention and attempting to surmount the insurmountable. I noticed that he was becoming increasingly angry. Finally I spoke.

'I suppose we'd be safe if we made absolutely sure that "Ivory" was spelt with a capital "I" and/or had inverted commas either side of it. That would imply a colour or possibly a manufacturer's name. If, however, we include the property in a newspaper advertisement, and if they then spell it with a small "i" we'd be back to the elephants' tusks problem again. We'd be held responsible, not the local rag.'

I observed that Mr. Bradshaw's face was turning an interesting shade of pink. I almost weakened but decided to stick to my guns.

'No, sorry. It's just too risky. We'll have to think of another way to describe your bathroom. Any ideas?'

He sighed heavily.

'I suppose we could call it off-white,' he said grudgingly.

I was horrified.

'Certainly not,' I replied. 'We live in an era of political correctness when everybody is ultra-sensitive. The term, "off-white" has racial overtones. Persons of ethnic origin could be deeply offended. We've already stopped saying "coloured" for the same reason.'

I warmed to my theme.

'Our mailing list is made up of hundreds of people of all shapes, sizes and colours and from all walks of life,' I explained. 'It's a microcosm of society, really, and I have to be extremely careful not to upset anyone.'

'All right, all right,' he said, his face becoming positively florid. 'What about "cream"?'

'No way,' I replied. 'If my mailing list contains any vegans, they'd find that word extremely offensive. I.......'

I didn't have time to finish before he grabbed me by the scruff of the neck and dragged me along the hall. I refused to give up.

'How about "Sort of yellowish?" I choked. 'We could say "bathroom with a sort of yellowish suite, radiator, double glazing and fitted carpet."

'That's hardly likely to sell the property is it?' he grunted, as he yanked the front door open. "Sort of yellowish suite," indeed!'

The door slammed shut. I picked myself up from the driveway, extracting bits of gravel from the knees of my best suit.

'It's not my fault!' I called through the letter box. 'I'm just trying to comply with The Property Misdescriptions Act. We get the same sort of problem with Avocado!'

I was wasting my breath. I could hear him speaking into the telephone.

'Is that Yookay Property Services? Good, I want to put my bungalow on the market.'

CHAPTER 6

Realisation

The mornings in my house are chaotic. We all have to leave at different times and the bathroom is therefore permanently engaged between the hours of seven and eight thirty. It just needs one person to get up late or to take longer than usual for the whole system to collapse into farce. A routine has evolved over the years whereby everyone has their set time in the bathroom and I use it last, having escaped the pandemonium by taking the dog for a walk.

Following this useful (for both of us) exercise, I return to my abode to find the bathroom, hopefully, unoccupied. The disadvantage, as far as I am concerned, is that the only available towels are laying in a sodden heap on the floor following the mass exodus. The room is also devoid of soap, shampoo, flannels and combs. Not only that, my razor is frequently blunt, having been used by one of the female members of the family for shaving legs. Apart from that, everything works perfectly.

Having got up at my usual time one morning and taken the dog for his customary romp in the woods, I returned home, had breakfast and went for a shower. The bathroom was in its usual state of disorder and I picked up a half empty bottle of shampoo which was laying on its side and leaking all over the shower tray. I looked at the label. Apparently, it was packed with vitamins, extracts of avocado, coconut oil and wheatgerm. I stood there wondering whether I should rub it into my scalp or drink it, when I noticed a statement at the bottom. 'BRINGS BACK

BEAUTIFUL HAIR,' it boasted. I was astounded. Most of my own 'beautiful hair' had disappeared down the plug-hole during the past few years and now here, at last, was the product I had been waiting for. 'By what miracle of science is this possible?' I wondered as I frantically massaged the concoction into my scalp. My hopes were dashed as I watched a few more hairs float towards the plug-hole. It was extremely disappointing that the shampoo was incapable of living up to its extravagant claims, and I left the shower feeling that I had been badly betrayed.

I managed to find a fine toothed comb which had been purchased some years earlier during an outbreak of head lice at the primary school. It was no longer needed for nit-searching but I was glad it had not been thrown away. I used it to re-arrange my sparse thatch into some semblance of order, still feeling somewhat peeved.

On the way to the office that morning, I passed the travel agents and glanced in the window. A card proclaimed 'BELGIUM - £195.' I stopped in my tracks. It was a moment or two before I realised they were offering a week's holiday at this price and were not actually trying to sell the entire country.

I carried on walking towards the office, feeling rather worried about my reaction to these trivial matters. For some reason, I was beginning to take everything too literally. Of course the shampoo manufacturers meant their product would improve the appearance of hair; of course the travel agents were only selling holidays and not entire countries!

As I sat down at my desk, the telephone rang. Cindy told me it was my old friend, Frank, and put him through. I was in no mood for one of Frank's complaining sessions about having to deal with endless reports and memo's or some of the nonsensical meetings he was obliged to attend. I was therefore rather abrupt and asked him what he wanted.

'Well,' he said hesitantly, 'I've got a bit of a problem,

actually.'

'I'm sorry, Frank,' I said. 'I've got to show someone over a house shortly. Perhaps I could call you later.'

I put the phone down and went off to show a Mr. & Mrs. Biggins over 9, Mafeking Terrace. We arrived within two minutes of each other and I did my best to find something good to say about the property. They already knew from my particulars that the place needed total renovation, but it was still a bit of a shock for them. Mr. Biggins said that he would have preferred to have seen running water coming out of the one tap in the house, rather than down the living room walls.

When I came back half an hour later, I felt rather guilty about having been so terse with Frank, and rang him back. He happened to answer the phone. When he had been self-employed he had always picked up the receiver and said 'Frank Lee speaking,' which had been faintly amusing when heard for the first time but extremely irritating after the umpteenth repetition.

Although he had been in the business for 25 years, his employers had seen fit to send him on a course instructing him on the complexities of answering the telephone.

'Good morning. Thank you for being kind enough to call Far & Wide Property Services. It really is a lovely day. Frank speaking, how may I help be of service?'

I waited patiently until he had finally stopped blathering.

'Good grief, man,' I exploded. 'You haven't just been trained, you've been run down by an Inter-City Express!'

'It's not my fault,' he grumbled apologetically. 'It's company policy.'

'I don't doubt it,' I told him, 'but it's just as well I'm not ringing from Australia. The call would have cost me a fortune! Do me a favour, though. Please, please, don't tell me to have a nice day when you ring off. That's all I ask.'

He promised faithfully that he would not do so now that he knew who was calling. My attitude softened to some extent and I asked him why he had telephoned earlier.

'Well, I feel a bit silly mentioning it,' he said, 'but the fact is that I think I've got some sort of mental disorder.'

'How do you mean?' I asked.

'Well, I just can't stop taking every statement, verbal or written, literally. Every time I see or hear a figure of speech, for example, I can't help taking it at face value!'

'Well, blow me down!' I exclaimed.

A puffing noise emanated from the telephone receiver and I realised that his problem was even more acute than my own.

'I'm having the same sort of trouble!' I told him, and related my experiences of that very morning.

I was glad I was not suffering alone and we both sat in silence for a few moments wondering what had happened to us. Suddenly, realisation came to us simultaneously.

'It's the Property Misdescriptions Act!' we exclaimed together.

We had, at last, realised that the strain of trying to comply with the uncompliable had taken its toll. We both considered ourselves to be conscientious people and had taken every possible precaution to avoid antagonising anyone. Now we were paying for it in the most extraordinary way!

Frank sounded particularly miserable and I did my best to console him.

'I've always tried to do my job without upsetting people,' he moaned. 'And now I'm constantly worrying about being reported to the Trading Standards Office. I'm sure I was right about the Taxpayers' Money Mountain.'

I ignored the last remark.

'I expect the whole thing will settle down,' I said soothingly. 'The Trading Standards people have far more important things to deal with. They're probably short staffed and will channel their efforts into something more worthwhile, given time.'

'I wish I could share your optimism,' he said. 'I'm just

waiting to make some trivial error and then they'll be down on me and Far & Wide Property Services like a ton of bricks. We'll both be persecuted!'

'Don't you mean "prosecuted?" I asked.

'I know what I mean!' he muttered grimly.

This was getting us nowhere. We were both suffering from hyper-active imagination triggered by the Property Misdescriptions Act and didn't know how to handle it. I thought it might help if he talked about his experiences.

'How have you been affected by all this?' I asked.

'I don't want to talk about it over the phone,' he said. 'How about a pint at lunchtime?'

I thought that was an excellent suggestion. I agreed to meet him at a suitable hostelry roughly mid-way between our two towns. I arrived at the pub a few minutes before Frank, bought a drink and looked around at my surroundings. Although we met occasionally at this particular venue, I had not been there since it had changed hands three weeks earlier. I was a little surprised to notice that the name had been altered from the King's Arms to the Monarch's Arms but, apart from that, nothing appeared to have changed.

The couple behind the bar were a rather intense couple in their thirties, although quite pleasant and eager to please. I sat down in an armchair next to the fire and glanced through the bar menu. It was the usual fare but I was momentarily puzzled by a note on the bottom directing my attention to the 'chalkboard' for the special dishes of the day. What on earth was a 'chalkboard' I wondered, and then the proverbial penny dropped. The item I had always understood to be a blackboard had been re-named in this establishment, presumably to avoid causing offence.

I sighed.

Was this sort of thing really necessary? Would any customer with African ancestors really be offended by the word 'blackboard' or would he or she burst out laughing at the ludicrous substitution? I suspected the latter would be the case. I was about to be mischievous and complain about the whitebait on the menu and suggest they changed it to 'chalkbait,' when Frank came in, which is probably just as well.

I bought Frank a drink and we ordered some lunch. We sat down in front of the fire and I encouraged Frank to tell me more about his experiences with our bizarre affliction.

'Like you, I've always done my best to avoid misleading people,' he said. 'Owners have complained when I've left things out of the particulars that they wanted put in. I've kept on demanding to see receipts for work carried out. They've either lost them or can't be bothered to find them. Then they've wanted to know why I don't believe them! It's a vicious circle!'

I quickly interrupted as he paused for breath. Frank was inclined to ramble on, as I may have already mentioned.

'We've all had that experience,' I said. 'Is there any particular incident you find worrying?'

Before he had a chance to reply, the landlady appeared with our meal. She smiled brightly at me.

'Are you the Ploughpersons' Lunch?' she enquired.

I resisted the temptation to ask whether I looked like a Ploughpersons' Lunch.

'Yes, thank you,' I said, 'and my friend is having the Sheepminders' pie with garden peas and baby carrots, organically grown on the premises.'

'I hope you don't mind my mentioning it,' I added, acting on a sudden impulse, 'but I don't think the name of my dish is very suitable.'

The smile froze on her face and a dangerous glint came into her eyes. She had taken the bait, having wrongly anticipated the reason for my apparent objection. Frank looked as if he wished he was somewhere else.

'I think the term "Ploughpersons' Lunch" is rather degrading and patronising to Ploughpersons everywhere,' I explained. 'It seems to suggest that they're peasants incapable of appreciating anything more adventurous than lumps of bread and cheese.'

The expression on her face changed to one of concern.

'I see what you mean,' she said thoughtfully. 'What do you think it ought to be called?'

I gave the matter a few moments consideration.

'How about "Cheddargorgers' Lunch?" I suggested. 'I can't see any problem with that. The Cheddar Gorge, being an inanimate object, is unlikely to raise many objections. I suppose it's possible that a group of humans naming itself "Friends of the Cheddar Gorge" might involve itself but that's a chance you'll just have to take.'

She hurried away to the 'chalkboard,' picked up a damp cloth and proceeded to obliterate the offending item.

Frank gave me a disapproving look.

'I do wish you wouldn't keep winding people up,' he said. 'It's so embarrassing.'

'Well,' I said, 'I'm sorry, but I do get fed up with all this political correctness. Most of it seems completely potty to me.'

'I agree,' he said. 'In fact that's given me an idea; it ought to be called "pottical correctness" really!'

We started eating our lunch.

'The menu's a bit misleading,' I commented, changing the subject slightly. 'The vegetables are supposed to be grown on the premises.'

'So?' he said.

'So, whereabouts on the premises?' I asked, and peered exaggeratedly under bar stools, searching for imaginary cauliflower and broccoli.

'You're right,' he said. 'Garden peas are, by definition, grown outside. You can't grow them on the premises; if you do, they're not garden peas, they're some other kind of pea.'

He paused, and a look of awareness came over his face. 'If, for example, they grew them in the bathroom, they ought to call them "bath-tub peas."

'Precisely,' I agreed, 'but I can't really imagine the

landlady asking her husband to remove the Grow-Bags before she takes a bath.'

We carried on eating in silence.

After a while, he gestured towards his plate with his knife.

'That's misleading, too.' he said.

'What?' I asked.

'Baby carrots,' he said. 'Even I know that carrots don't have babies. At least, I've never seen anyone pushing a carrot down the road in a pram.'

'It would be cruel and heartless to take them away from their mothers if they did have babies,' I pointed out. 'They're just small.'

'I expect they're undersized ones that the supermarkets have rejected,' he agreed.

'I always thought that pubs are governed by fairly stringent rules and regulations,' I said. 'I'm surprised that this place has got away with all these misdescriptions. That reminds me. You were going to tell me about your experiences since the Property Misdescriptions Act came into force.'

'Well, they're much the same as yours,' he answered. 'I started by deleting all adjectives from my particulars, made sure photographs were not misleading, told all the staff not to voice any opinions whatsoever about any property and thought that would cover it.'

'But your problems didn't stop there, I'm sure.' I said.

'That's right. I always send sales particulars to vendors for approval and one of them came back wanting to know why there was a white blob on the photograph of his house.'

I was puzzled.

'And what was it?' I asked.

'Well, I hadn't noticed it at the time, but next door's cat had wandered into the shot and I had to Tippex it out of the photograph. If I hadn't, a prospective purchaser could have travelled hundreds of miles to view, expecting to get "Sooty" included in the sale of the house.'

I sympathised. 'I had the same sort of problem when I

photographed a bungalow near the US Air Force base. An F16 fighter plane came into view just as I released the shutter. I had to take another photograph.'

We seemed to have got slightly off the subject again, due to Franks inclination to digress. I tried a different approach.

'I believe you recently went on a training course,' I said. 'How did you get on?'

'Which one do you mean?' he asked. 'I went to the half day one about answering the telephone last Tuesday, the one about preparing and receiving memo's on Thursday morning and the all-day one on Friday. That was a full programme covering various items including economies, the Property Misdescriptions Act and increasing our market share.'

'Let's go for that one, then,' I said, and settled back in my armchair resigning myself to an hour long monologue. Frank was not easily distracted once he got into his stride. I had already heard the preamble many times before and I was about to hear it again.

CHAPTER 7

Market Day

The regional director of Far & Wide Property Services had organised the training meeting for the whole day on the previous Friday. Since the heady days of the property market boom and the subsequent inevitable decline, meetings had become ever more frequent. The thinking behind it appeared to be that the only way to become profitable again was to bombard the staff with memo's and organise lots of seminars.

The regional director was known to all and sundry by his initials, L.C. Following a career in the army, he had decided, on retirement, to join Boggs, Son and Whiffle, a small long-established estate agency being run by his cousin. The original Boggs and his son had been rag and bone men who had originally done their business from door to door in the town and had later been joined by Jeremiah Whiffle who had been an auctioneer selling livestock in the market.

From these humble beginnings they had built up a sound estate agency business and their offspring had taken over from them when they'd retired. The 'son' had, in fact, retired ten years before L.C. joined them and had had illusions of grandeur and self-importance. This was probably due to the fact that he had walked into the business without having the inconvenience of building it up by himself.

Boggs, Son and Whiffle had been acquired by the Far & Wide Property Services chain, which in itself, had been put together by the Far & Wide Building Society three years earlier. The Chief Executive had purchased a map of the British Isles and divided it up into squares with a ruler and a red ballpoint pen. He had identified Boggs, Son & Whiffle's territory as one of the pieces still missing from his jigsaw puzzle and had offered an absurdly large sum of money for it. L.C.'s cousin, realising that the intrinsic value of an estate agency office lies not in the fabric but in the management, metaphorically snapped his hand off and promptly went into retirement in warmer climes.

L.C. was not yet ready for retirement and had ambitions of power. He was a tall, distinguished-looking middle aged man, always immaculately dressed in blue pin-striped suit, regimental tie and highly polished black shoes. His perfectly laundered, snowy white shirt would have been the pride of any washing powder manufacturer.

As a result of his military training, he soon earned a reputation for being a first class motivator of men and women and was rapidly promoted, firstly to area manager and eventually to regional director. It was generally acknowledged that it would not be too long before he replaced the chief executive himself.

L.C.'s advancement, however, was not entirely popular with the existing staff since he had gained the reputation of being a hatchet man for the company. If any individuals were not performing to the high standards insisted upon, L.C. would be the one to sack them with the minimum notice required by law. He was also responsible for opening and closing branches. Any office failing to reach the profitability target for two months running was likely to find the furniture removal van pulling up outside one Friday afternoon.

Staff soon came to realise that they crossed L.C. at their peril. Tales of his swift revenge were legendary, although, no doubt somewhat exaggerated. One of these stories involved a manager whose office was performing well below target. His car was now three years old, had done more than 70,000 miles and, despite the numerous hints he had dropped on every possible occasion, there was no sign of it being replaced. He had therefore had the temerity to send a memo to L.C., demanding a car of a standard commensurate with his hard work and ability and reflecting his value to the firm. L.C. was not amused. He was accustomed to making demands and giving orders, not accepting them.

Acting on his instructions, L.C.'s secretary/P.A., Doreen, had telephoned the manager telling him to expect a replacement car the very next day. He was to hand the keys of his present one over to his assistant who had just passed her driving test.

The following day, the great man himself had arrived driving a top of the range Volvo, put his head round the door of the office and asked the manager to come outside. When he had done so, L.C. handed over the keys to a 10 year old Skoda which had been following on behind, driven by Doreen. L.C. and Doreen had promptly driven off in the Volvo and the manager, realising that his career prospects with the Company were virtually non-existent, took the hint and spent the rest of the afternoon scouring the situations vacant columns in the local paper.

L.C. thoroughly enjoyed organising staff meetings and training sessions. It gave him the opportunity of reminding them who was boss and he revelled in the limelight. He was accompanied everywhere by Doreen, an elegant widow in early middle age who was highly efficient and possessed an awesome memory. Rumours were naturally rife about these two and people suspected, without any justification whatsoever, that she took down more than just shorthand.

Some wag had unkindly dubbed Doreen 'L.C.'s Widow of Opportunity.' This was a snide reference to L.C.'s ever-increasing fondness for using buzz words and jargon. He had always had a reputation for using clear and concise English until he had reached his forty fifth birthday. He had then made a conscious effort to show everyone he came into contact with that he was still youthful and 'with it.' The result was that he now spoke fluent gibberish which few people understood, least of all the staff, most of whom were half his age.

The training session was well under way on this particular occasion and Frank appeared to hang on L.C.'s every word. He had, however, mastered the technique of sleeping with his eyes open. It was not that he was lazy; it was simply that, rightly or wrongly, he considered he knew more about the business than L.C did and, secondly, he had no idea what he was talking about.

L.C. was gazing aloofly at the fifty or so staff assembled in front of him, flanked by the faithful Doreen on one side and her young assistant Justin, on the other. L.C. was concluding his opening speech, which had lasted a good hour.

'At the end of the day,' he was saying, 'it's a whole new ball game out there. Having said that, the way forward is under active consideration and, as a major player, Far & Wide Property Services take on board that it's a level playing field opportunity-wise.'

Staff members were gazing back at him with rapt attention and one or two were nodding sagely. They had not understood a word.

'Questions?' demanded L.C. tersely.

Everyone stared back blankly and the silence was becoming rather unnerving. Finally, one of the least experienced assistant managers hesitantly put up his hand.

'Some sections of the Trade Press are saying that Yookay Property Services is ahead of us profit-wise. Is it true, L.C?'

L.C. glared at him.

'I hear what you say, Dean. They may have been flavour of the month last year, but their strategy is fatally flawed. They've had a number of cold starts recently, but the writing's on the wall and I believe our conversion rate is greater than theirs but the jury's still out on that one.'

Dean was totally baffled by this answer, but had the wit to realise that he should have kept quiet. He suspected, quite correctly, that his lack of judgement had been noted. This was confirmed when L.C added menacingly, 'No Brownie points for that one, Dean.'

Dean cringed back in his seat and said nothing more for the rest of the day.

L.C. was not entirely surrounded by sycophants, however, Frank being one of the few exceptions. I liked Frank. He was a thoroughly decent man and devoted to his business; what he didn't know about the property market wasn't worth knowing. He was, however, incredibly näive in his private life and inclined to be a little bit of a bore. He had been married, but his wife had left him several years earlier. I well remembered the sad tale he had told me about their parting.

He had gone along to the Rotary Club one Thursday evening, as he invariably did, and someone had reminded him that it was his turn to find a speaker to give a short talk after the meal. Frank had completely forgotten about it and was told that, in that case, he must do the job himself. Frank had never been keen on public speaking and had reluctantly returned home to fetch his collection of foreign beer bottle labels to use as a basis for his talk.

Upon arriving home, Frank had been somewhat surprised to find the house deserted downstairs and even more bewildered to discover his wife upstairs in bed with another man.

Frank had demanded an explanation and the man had told him that he had been calling randomly at houses in the neighbourhood, engaged in carrying out important market research for his employers, the Acme Bed Company. He had explained that it had been imperative for Frank's wife to lay next to him for the in-depth analysis to be of any value.

Frank couldn't believe his luck. He had immediately

abandoned the search for his beer bottle labels and insisted that the inspector for ABC should stop work for the evening and accompany him back to the Rotary Club in order to give a short talk about his job.

'It was a bit of a let-down really,' Frank had told me. 'There I was, really pleased at not having to give a talk and all he did was keep looking at his watch all through the meal. In the end, he remembered an urgent appointment and dashed off.'

Frank had then had a few drinks at the bar afterwards and returned home feeling rather deflated. Another surprise had been in store for him. His wife had left a note for him on the kitchen table saying she had decided to emigrate to the Isle Of Wight. He never saw her again.

'I'm so sorry,' I said. 'Whatever did you do?'

'Well,' he replied, 'I couldn't see any point in replacing the bed after that, so I wrote to ABC demanding my £100 deposit back. I'm not that stupid.'

The point had been debatable but I let it go. Since that time, his fortunes had literally improved when Far and Wide had made him an offer for his business that he couldn't refuse. They kept him on as area manager for his former offices on a three years contract. He ran the branches with his customary expertise despite L.C.'s efforts to institutionalise him.

L.C. had disliked Frank on sight. He knew that he had been in the business for longer than he had and would have liked to have got rid of him. He was also aware that Frank had received a considerable sum of money when F & W had acquired his business. It was therefore likely that Frank could have retired had he chosen to do so; such a man was unlikely to be browbeaten into anything and therefore didn't fit in with L.C.'s plans. In view of the three year contract and the fact that Frank had enough money to be financially independent, he would have been completely unaffected by any threats that L.C. could make and therefore L.C., realising this, desisted from making any.

Frank also had the habit of making seemingly innocent remarks which tended to disrupt meetings and undermined L.C.'s authority. L.C. suspected, quite correctly, that this was done simply to annoy him.

L.C. once informed staff at a training session that F & W were going to update their sales literature and start using modern measurements. There was an immediate response from Frank, who was in the habit of referring to L.C. either as 'Elsie' or 'El Cid,' as the mood took him.

'Does that mean we're going to have to stop measuring land in rods, perches and poles?' he enquired.

L.C had treated him to a look of pure venom.

'No, it does not,' he muttered through clenched teeth and then quickly corrected himself. 'Of course we're not and no-one's done so for fifty years, as you well know. We're going metric.'

He was aware of suppressed laughter from the other staff members and hated being made to look a fool. He frantically wondered for the tenth time that day how he could get rid of Frank. He resolved to buttonhole him during the break and try to interest him in early retirement. Unbeknown to him, Frank thoroughly enjoyed his job and saw no point in retiring to sit around an empty house all day long. Training meetings were a source of comic relief to him and made a welcome change to normal office routine.

It was time for the first item on the agenda. A training manager stood by a flip-chart, marker pen poised. On the right-hand side he listed numerous items under the heading 'outgoings' and on the other side he wrote 'income.' He then informed everyone present that in order to make a profit, it was necessary that the annual figures achieved in the left-hand column should exceed the total incurred in the right. Several pairs of eyes swivelled round to look at Frank, but he was oblivious, having entered a trance-like state. The trainer carried on scribbling on his flip-chart for half an hour and then other speakers came and went. Staff asked inane questions at regular intervals until the coffee-break.

The staff meandered through to an ante-room where the refreshments were being served. Having obtained their cups of coffee and biscuits, they stood around chatting. Frank circulated from group to group just managing to keep ahead of Elsie, who was determined to catch him and have a few words without it looking too obvious. One of the instructors announced that the next session was about to start and everyone went back to their places. Frank noticed with some satisfaction that Elsie was looking rather frustrated.

Everyone was settling down again after the break when L.C. took the floor and announced that he was now going to talk to everyone about setting out their stalls in the market place. Frank sat bolt upright. Had he misjudged Elsie? He suddenly realised that he was about to hear a master plan of stunning audacity; one that was going to revolutionise the business and bring the company back into profit again!

They were all going to vacate their offices and each have a barrow in their respective market towns!

'Brilliant!' Frank thought. 'The man's a genius, after all!'

There would be no more exorbitant rents to pay, no more crushing business rates and most other overheads would be cut to the bone. Frank's already over-developed imagination went into overdrive and a clear vision came unbidden into his mind:

Elsie was standing behind a barrow in the town centre, but something about his appearance had changed. He was still wearing his customary pin-stripe suit trousers but the jacket had been flung over one of the handles of the barrow. The knot of his regimental tie had been loosened and his shirt sleeves were rolled up to the elbows. He was calling out to passers-by but something had also happened to his speech. His normally well-modulated tones had given way to a 'Sarf London' accent.

'Get your 'ouses 'ere, they're luvvley!' he bawled.' 'I've got two bed 'ouses in tahn, 3 bed bungalows in the suburbs, 4 bed country 'ouses and a ten bed mansion wiv garages for three rollers!'

His eagle eye spotted a young woman trudging along, a heavy shopping bag in each hand and two toddlers clinging to her coat sleeves. His unwavering intuition told him that she needed more space than her present abode provided and that she was probably still living in the parental home.

''ow about you missus?' he yelled. 'I've got a nice 3 bedder 'ere. Gas central 'eating and garage! Fresh in terday!'

A crowd started to gather round and was looking bemused. The young woman hesitated and Elsie knew he was in with a chance. He picked up a set of particulars in his left hand and held his right aloft, gaining the attention of the crowd.

'I'm not askin' £99,950,' he bellowed. 'I'm not askin' £79,950!'

An expectant hush fell over the crowd.

With a theatrical flourish, Elsie brought his right hand down from on high, slapping the leaflet in his left. 'Give me £59,950 and I'll throw in a one bedroom retirement flat for yer granny!'

The young woman was elbowed aside as the crowd surged forward, eager to take advantage of this stupendous offer.

To no-one in particular, Elsie added, 'I'm a fool to meself, I really am,' and then called over to his long-suffering secretary.

'Chuck them keys over, Doreen!' He leered at the audience. 'Luvvley gel that, ladies 'n' gentlemen, luvvley gel!'

The audience automatically glanced over at Doreen, who was looking rather dishevelled and far from her normally immaculate self. She was perspiring freely and a stray lock of hair hung over one eye. It was hardly surprising, since she was sitting astride a contraption rather like an exercise bicycle connected up to a portable generator supplying electricity to her typewriter. A cigarette dangled from the corner of her mouth. She was pedalling furiously and typing simultaneously at the rate of 120 words per minute. She stopped typing but her feet barely slowed down as she rummaged around in a drawer attached to the underside of the barrow.

Noticing Elsie's lecherous gaze in her direction, she gave him a coy sidelong look in return. She tossed the house keys over to him and, as her hand completed the movement, her fingers formed a rude gesture.

Elsie just grinned and turned to his young assistant, Justin. 'Go and show the punters 'round the gaffe son,' he murmured. 'Don't come back 'til you've sold it and bring me back a sausage sandwich from the caff.'

As an afterthought, he continued, 'When you've got the buyer lined up and fixed the mortgage, go and see Roger, sharpish. He'll get the legal side sorted.'

This was a reference to the solicitor leaning on the next barrow and shouting, 'Get your conveyancing here....... wills drawn up while you wait......!'

The glazed expression on Frank's face slowly faded as he heard his name being called. A colleague was tapping him on the shoulder and informing him that it was lunch-time. He wandered out of the room in a daze, feeling worried about his constant daydreaming. At this rate, he would soon be completely detached from reality. He desperately wondered how to overcome this strange affliction.

CHAPTER 8

Gone to the Dogs

Frank sat back in his armchair looking drained after the account he had just given. I went to the bar and ordered another pint of best bitter each and watched closely as Frank consumed a considerable amount. This seemed to revive his spirits to some extent.

'Well, you're certainly suffering at the moment,' I told him. 'What you need is a good holiday! Either that, or you need to take medical advice.'

'I only came back from holiday two weeks ago,' he reminded me. 'And I haven't got much faith in doctors.'

I resolved to mention Frank's peculiar malady to a doctor acquaintance of mine next time I saw him. At that moment, a couple came into the bar with a small dog of indeterminate breed and sat down at the next table. If there's anything that irritates me more than the Property Misdescriptions Act at the moment, it's dogs. I don't dislike all dogs, of course, that would be unreasonable. My own Springer Spaniel is perfectly well behaved. It's just other people's dogs that I can't abide. If only they would just leave me alone. I do my best to ignore them but they either love me or hate me. There's just nothing in between. This particular dog, for example, proved that love at first sight is not a fallacy and proceeded to have a meaningful relationship with my right leg. Since its owners obviously had no control over it whatsoever, I hurriedly said goodbye to Frank, explaining that I had some appointments to attend to, and left him to deal with the ardent attentions of Fido.

I had a pleasant drive back to the town and went straight to 9, Mafeking Terrace. I was due to meet a jobbing builder there and waited until he arrived. He was in business in a small way and bought a run-down property occasionally to keep himself and his son occupied when trade was slack. They would then put it on the market and hoped to make a modest profit.

Whilst I was waiting for him to arrive, I had a quick look around. The property was rapidly deteriorating. At one time, I would probably have described it as a 'home with an income'; any enterprising purchaser could have gathered a good crop of mushrooms each morning from under the kitchen sink and from the cupboard under the stairs, and then sold them to local restaurateurs.

I heard a van pull up outside and rushed out to meet the builder. I didn't want to be still inside the house when he banged on the front door; it just wouldn't be safe.

He had a quick look over the property and said he would want the owner to pay him to take it off her hands. I said that was unlikely to be of interest and we parted company. Since estate agents are obliged by law to put all offers in writing at the soonest possible moment, I wrote to the solicitors with his proposal. They didn't bother to waste a stamp on a reply.

I set off for my next appointment, not looking forward to it at all, since the house was not in a very salubrious part of town. I parked in between two ancient rusting heaps outside the crumbling terraced house and was approached by half a dozen ten year olds who had been lurking about nearby. One of them offered to look after my car. Apparently this service would cost me three pounds and I suggested that he and his friends should go away, in language they would readily understand.

From first glance, the house appeared to be a fairly typical Victorian property and a plaque over the front door bearing the date '1866' seemed to confirm this. I wrote down 'Victorian Villa' on my clipboard.

Warning bells sounded in the back of my mind. Since the Property Misdescriptions Act came into force it was necessary to heed the advice to 'exercise all due diligence' at all times.

I was having problems with the word 'villa.' To many people this word could conjure up images of relaxing by a swimming pool and sipping sangria in the sunshine; very misleading in this particular street. I crossed out 'villa' and substituted 'house.'

Again I hesitated. Was the house really Victorian? Was it possible that it had been built in 1066 and that some vandal had altered the nought into an eight? I peered up at the plaque shortsightedly, having inadvertently left my glasses at the office.

Still unsure, I thought it best not to take any chances. I crossed out 'Victorian' and wrote down 'old.' I paused yet again. What constituted 'old?' Since umpteen million years have elapsed since the 'Big Bang,' a hundred, or even a thousand, years seemed fairly recent. I scrubbed everything out, except the word 'house.'

I walked up the path, stepping over an abandoned pram, a skateboard and other accumulated rubbish. There was a general air of decay about the place. I knocked tentatively on the front door and all hell broke loose; deep throated barks, much door slamming and shouting issued from the interior. I backed away slightly as the front door was eventually opened. I groaned inwardly; as I had already anticipated, it was the sort of household where it would be necessary to wipe my feet on the way out.

The house-holder stood in the doorway wearing filthy jeans. A greasy t-shirt full of holes revealed a tattooed dotted line around the throat with the instructions 'cut here' below it. A can of lager clutched in one hand and a cigarette dangling from the other completed the picture.

I found myself in a bit of a quandary. Should I stay and discuss marketing strategy, terms of business etc. now, or come back later when her husband was in from work? Events then took place which made up my mind for me.

I could hear menacing guttural snarls coming from the interior and the unmistakable sound of claws scrabbling against the linoleum. Peering past the owner into the gloom, I could just make out a dog lead. One end was attached to what appeared to be the family pit bull, whilst the other was being grasped by a little girl of about four years old. As I watched, she gave up the unequal struggle and let go of her end of the lead.

I returned to the car in a time Linford Christie would have been proud of, assisted by the skateboard which happened to be in my path.

I sat in the front seat panting whilst the Pet from Hell attacked the car with all the ferocity of the Hound of the Baskervilles. My client addressed the animal in fluent Anglo-Saxon. It gave me a last malevolent glare before slinking back into the house, furious at having been denied its prey. The owner turned her attention to me.

'What about me free valuation?' she yelled. I looked at her and wondered whether she was a member of the local Neighbourhood Witch scheme. Not wanting to risk opening the car door, I called out through the closed window.

'I've just realised that your property is a little outside my normal area,' I told her. 'I'm afraid I won't be able to accept instructions to deal with it after all.'

I had a sudden inspiration and added, 'Why not ring Floggitt & Quick? I'm sure they will be delighted to help you. Be sure to ask for Daryl.'

She turned on her heel without uttering another word, and went back into the house, slamming the door behind her.

Grateful for my lucky escape, I turned the key in the ignition and eased my foot down on the accelerator. The engine roared but the car remained stationary. As I checked that the hand brake was off, a movement in the distance caught my eye. A group of small boys was running along, bowling what appeared to be large hoops along the road.

Understanding dawned. I wound down the window, peered out and my worst fears where confirmed. I saw that a neat pile of bricks stood at each corner of the car where the wheels had once been. In the circumstances, I did the only thing possible.

I hummed a few bars of 'Air on a G-string' and lit up a small cigar.

CHAPTER 9

'Deer Cur........'

Luckily, a passing police patrol car had noticed my predicament and came to my rescue. Having heard my account of the story, they went off in pursuit with their siren blaring. They were back within ten minutes and a short time later my car enjoyed a reunion with its four wheels. The lads, needless to say, had scarpered.

I returned to the office and settled myself in my room before interviewing a new trainee receptionist who was about to leave school. Cindy ushered her into my room and she told me that her name was Michelle. She was neatly dressed, very presentable and self-assured.

'I expect your careers teacher sent you here today, Michelle,' I began.

'Yeah,' she responded. ''e goes, "There's a job goin' at the Estate Agents." I go "yeah?" 'e goes "Yeah," I go, "What do I do?" 'e goes, "Go for an interview." I go, "When?" 'e goes "I've fixed it for 'alf past two." I'm goin' "Mega"!'

All this had been delivered excitedly at increasing speed and volume. It reminded me of a runaway train, not that I had ever encountered one. If I ever do, however, I am sure that it will sound just like Michelle. I felt slightly dazed as she paused for breath and I took the opportunity of getting the proverbial word in edgeways.

'How did he go......., I mean, what did he say then?' I hurriedly corrected myself. '

''e goes, "Tell him about your GCSE's." I go.......'

'There's a vacancy here for a trainee receptionist cum

secretary,' I interrupted, not wishing for a repeat performance of the 'I go, 'e goes' routine.

'We need someone who is willing to learn and who has basic keyboard skills. The most important requirement is that I need someone with lots of enthusiasm.' She clearly had plenty of this and, since I felt that she had the potential to become a very conscientious employee, I agreed to let her start the following week.

Michelle arrived on Monday morning bright and early and I introduced her to the other members of staff. She was keen to learn and it was decided that she should type a few letters. She was given a tape, a transcriber complete with headphones and a pile of letterheads. We then left her to get on with it.

The word processor was equipped with a spellchecker which chimed each time it suspected a spelling mistake. Next time I passed the reception area where Michelle was working, the machine appeared to be making a fair attempt at playing 'Jingle Bells.' I decided it would be better not to intervene on her first morning and left her in peace.

Just before lunch time, Michelle proudly brought in her first letter. I asked her to sit down whilst I checked it through.

'Mr. J. William's   (it read)
63, Woodlands' Garden's,
Bury St. Edmunds',
S'uffolk.
Deer cur,
Thankyou for your leter from which I not that you are looking for a 4 bedroom house not to far from the town center. Ihave put your name on our maling list and if anything sootable come's on to our regjester's.......'

I stopped reading and attempted to explain the mystery of the musical word processor and the wonders of the wandering apostrophe. I then suggested that she went to lunch and borrowed a dictionary from Cindy afterward.

After the door had closed, I sat back in my chair and sighed. I read through Michelle's letter again and felt close to despair. This experience was not new to me; it was now normal practice for employers to try and fill in the gaping holes in young peoples' education.

I did not attach any blame to Michelle; she was certainly bright enough. It was hardly her fault if her teachers had not wanted to inhibit her self-expression by cluttering up her mind with formal spelling and basic punctuation!

I wondered whether any of the decision-makers in education ever regretted betraying Michelle, and others like her, with their so-called progressive ideas. Somehow, I doubted it. I suspected that their folly was exceeded only by their arrogance. I was willing to bet, however, that their own secretaries had been middle aged walking dictionaries.

I had a quiet word with the other staff who were keeping an eye on Michelle, showing her the filing systems and other office procedures. Although they now all used up-to-date office machinery, they had started on much more primitive models. At that time, their letters had been produced on typewriters loaded with top copy, carbon paper and flimsy paper for the file. Spelling errors were few and far between since they had to be removed by erasers which frequently left grubby marks on the letter, which was then promptly sent back by the person who had dictated it. This tended to concentrate the typist's mind so that she rarely made mistakes, avoiding the need to do the same letter over and over again.

Word processors have now dispensed with the need for precision typing since not a word is printed until the operator is satisfied with what appears on the screen. I'm not saying that we should go back to the old methods - far from it. I could not imagine trying to cope without a pocket calculator these days! Arithmetic has never been one of my strong points. Before the advent of these electronic wonders, I used to add up the petty cash several times and get several different answers. If two of them happened to coincide, I eagerly accepted it as being correct.

To return to Michelle, she had a very pleasant personality, liked meeting people and was anxious to do well in her job. All of these qualities are prerequisites in my business, as in any other, and I had every confidence that she would succeed.

If only we could get rid of the EastEnders accent.......!

CHAPTER 10

Microchips with everything

My first task, on arriving at the office the following morning, was to open the post. I was in quite a cheerful mood, having seen Darryl on the way to the office; he was limping painfully. I assumed he had met the Pet from Hell. I tossed the bills on one side, unopened, and concentrated on more interesting looking envelopes.

One letter was from the Yookay Building Society, inviting me to their annual Golf Tournament. I had not been to one before, made a note of it in my diary and wrote thanking them for the invitation. Another letter was from someone in London who was looking for a three bedroom country cottage with half an acre up to £30,000. I resisted the temptation to write back and ask him to let me know if he found any and I'd then have a couple as well. Instead, I sent a polite letter back saying we were not likely to have anything of interest coming onto our books in the near future and that he should try a little further northward. (I ignored the urge to add 'like the Orkney Islands').

The last item of post was the monthly stationery catalogue. I glanced through it and came across the office machine section. I never ceased to wonder at the range of electronic machines available. Telephones (with and without cards), voice-activated recorders, memory typewriters, personal publishing systems, photocopiers, laser copiers; the range was vast and seemingly endless. Suddenly, one particular item caught my eye. It was a combined spelling checker/thesaurus, with over five hundred thousand words, on offer at a very reasonable price. Judging from the blurb, this gadget would be even more reliable than the memory typewriter with spellchecker. Just the thing for our new junior, Michelle! No longer would I have to put up with mis-spelt letters; no more returning work for correction. Efficiency would improve and Michelle would feel a lot happier since the results of her hard work would no longer be sent back to her. I filled out the coupon and sent it through the fax without further delay.

The machine was delivered twenty four hours later. I inserted the batteries and read the instructions. I decided to test a few words I usually find troublesome. The correct spellings came up on the screen instantaneously! I tried another word and pressed the thesaurus button. The results were astonishing. An impressive list of synonyms appeared, one by one, simply by pressing the right key. Press another key and it would list words with spellings close to that of the word which had been entered. I was beginning to enjoy this. No wonder people became so hooked on computer games.

This sort of gadget is of course, taken for granted by my children but I was awestruck. Not only did this hand-held machine contain half a million words, but it was also able to assemble them into a seemingly infinite number of lists at the touch of a button. I wondered just how comprehensive this machine could be.

I typed in 'SUPERHETERODYNE.'

'CORRECT!' was the instant response.

I tried 'QUINQUENNIAL.'

'CORRECT!' was the immediate reply.

(Okay, I admit I cheated by finding them at random in the dictionary first.)

'Right, matey, let's see how clever you really are!' I thought

I entered the same word again, this time deliberately leaving out the last 'N', and pressed the ENTER key.

'WORKING.......' came up on the screen.

'QUINQUENNIAL....... QUINQUENNIALS........ QUINQUENNIALLY,' it churned out cockily, and threw in 'QUINTILLION' for good measure.

'Think you're damn' clever don't you?' I muttered grimly through clenched teeth. I was not going to be bettered by a machine and had a sudden inspiration. Acting on a rather childish impulse, I typed in a naughty word.

'WORKING.......' came up on the screen.

This time, a series of pulsating dots followed while it searched it's memory. Eventually, 'NOT A WORD' was displayed.

'That's odd,' I thought. 'I was watching a film on t.v last night and distinctly heard it several times. I bet it's just been censored.'

I tried another well used Americanism from the same film. Again, it examined its entire half million word vocabulary but, having no luck, displayed 'NOT A WORD' again. I pressed the thesaurus button to find out whether it would come up with any substitutes.

'DONKEYPIT' was the remarkable suggestion.

I couldn't really imagine Arnold Schwarzenegger using this particular insult and pressed ENTER again.

'MULEMINE' was the rather hopeful response.

I pressed ENTER several more times. It decided to try a different approach, using all the words it could think of beginning with 'AS.'

'ASHTRAY....... ASPIRIN....... ASSEGAI.......'

'Sorry, "Thez",' I said triumphantly. 'You're way off beam. You're really clutching at straws now!'

'ASSISTED PASSAGE....... ASTRAL BODY.......'

I began to feel quite sorry for it. There was an air of desperation about the pathetic attempts it was making.

'ASTRO-HATCH....... ASTROPHYSICS.......'

I decided to put it out of its misery before it had a nervous breakdown and switched it off.

'This is ridiculous,' I thought. 'Not only am I humanising

it by giving it a name, I'm also assuming it's capable of rational thought and having human illnesses!'

I had a brainwave. I realised what the problem must be. The machine had been made in Korea and the original had been developed for the USA using American English. This one had been produced for the British market, using English English. It had, therefore, been totally baffled by the idiom I had used. I put my theory to the test by tapping in a typically English crudity and activated the thesaurus button.

The machine went through the now familiar routine of producing pulsating dots; the electronic equivalent of scratching its head whilst wondering what to say next.

'GLOBES' was the helpful answer.

I rather liked that and decided to commit it to memory for future use. I switched the machine off again, put it down on the desk and considered the possibilities.

Every sports journalist and commentator ought to have one. On second thoughts, I realised that most sports writers already have one. Check the back page of any newspaper, for example, and you will find that footballers rarely kick the ball. They shoot, fire, strike, scorch or power it into the back of the net. They tap it in, hammer it in, sidefoot it, increase their tally, hit the target, double the lead or pull one back but they never seem to simply kick it.

I recently read that a player placed the ball on the spot and drove home. Presumably it was quicker than catching the bus and no doubt the substitute had to come on.

T.V commentators, however, do not appear to have any such assistance. They do an excellent job most of the time but, being human, do occasionally dry up.

'Not often enough,' I hear you say, uncharitably.

Be that as it may, they would find a thesaurus machine a real boon. Words would literally be at their fingertips.

Imagine the scene: it's a Saturday evening. Well known

sporting celebrities are sitting in a t.v studio watching a monitor and discussing a recorded match in depth. The host is mindful of his producer's instructions to use more imaginative and colourful language and has invested in an electronic thesaurus. Play has been interrupted and a player writhes in agony on the ground in front of the opposing goal.

The commentator looks suitably disapproving.

'He's sustained a nasty injury in the, um.......' He quickly checks his thesaurus. '........ in the globes, I fear. Seems to me to be a clear sending-off offence. What say you, Alan?'

'Och, there's noo doot in ma mind, Jimmy,' he says. 'The lad's played fantastic. He's got the ball, he's on his way tae goal and he's brought doon from behind.'

'Um, he's Jimmy and I'm Des,' the commentator says. He turns to his other colleague. 'What's your opinion, Jimmy? How did he do that?'

'It was a cynical off-the-ball tackle. The lad's played exceptional, he's got behind the defence and suddenly "whack!" and he's on the ground. It makes me sick! Early bath-time for the defender and a definite penalty, in my opinion!'

Alan chimes in again and is gesticulating indignantly.

'It's a definite goal. The striker's in the area, he's aboot tae deliver, he's brought doon an' it's goodnight Glasgae!'

'Vienna,' comments Jimmy.

'Wha'?'

'I think the expression is "Goodnight Vienna" not "Goodnight Glasgow."'

'Vienna, Glasgae, wha' the hell!'

Whilst off-camera, the commentator has taken the opportunity of expanding his vocabulary with the aid of his electronic friend.

'Yes, you're absolutely right, Jimmy,' he says. 'The referee's shown the defender the Red Card and he's pointing at the pimple!'

The defender has walked off the pitch and the 'lad,' a

thirty three year old father of three, immediately makes a remarkable recovery aided by the miraculous powers of the wet sponge which has just been slopped around his nether-regions. He places the ball on the penalty spot and carries on with his job.

I pause to wonder what the trainer puts in his bucket. Whatever it is, it ought to be available on the National Health. Waiting time in the local G.P.'s surgery would be dramatically reduced. You'd hardly have time to get the words, 'It's me piles Doctor,' out of your mouth before he'd be shoving an ice-cold dripping-wet sponge down your trousers.

The ball hits the back of the net. The commentator's fingers have been flying over the keys of his electronic box of tricks. He adopts an incredulous tone of voice.

Until now, he would have said, 'It's a goal! The home supporters are going absolutely wild!'

It now comes out as 'It's an objective! The bread-winners are becoming completely undomesticated!'

A knock on the door brought me out of my reverie. It was Michelle bringing in a cup of coffee. She was not always the one to make it, I hasten to add, in these politically correct times. I've even been known to make coffee for everyone myself when the office is busy. I'm not totally out of date!

I handed the new toy over to Michelle and explained that it was going to make her life, and mine, so much easier in the future.

'You'll have all the words you need at your fingertips,' I told her, and gave her a tape full of letters to type out.

'Here's a tape I prepared earlier,' I said jovially. 'Make sure you check every single word without fail on the spelling machine.'

'But I've already got a dictionary,' she protested.

'Chuck it in the bin!' I replied. 'It's not relevant in a modern stream-lined office like ours. It's old-fashioned.'

She still looked doubtful.

'Look,' I said. 'I'm older than you, but I'm willing to move with the times!'

She gave me a look which made me feel like Methuselah's grandfather.

'All you have to do,' I went on hurriedly, 'is to enter the word as it sounds. It will then list "correction candidates" and you just pick the one you want. It couldn't be easier.'

At last I felt confident that my letters would be faultlessly produced and I carried on with my normal business.

Towards the end of the day, a beaming Michelle came into my office carrying a folder full of completed letters under her arm. I was speaking on the telephone at the time and gave a cheery wave as she deposited them on my desk. She went out of the room and I eagerly opened the folder.

The first letter was a standard one which we send to Vendors thanking them for their instructions to sell their properties and asking for confirmation that our description sheet is correct. It read as follows:-

> 'Dire Madman,
> I rite to thank you for kindly inducting me to plaice your property on my re jesters at £87,950. I enclose a draught copy of our particulars. Wood you please cheque them carefully for eros and confer that they are correct. Under the Property Misdirections Axe, I will be unable to sail your hearse unless I have your constipation within three days.
>
> Yours fatuously,'

I sat quietly for a few moments digesting what I had just read, elbows on desk, head in hands. I closed my eyes in concentration. Somehow, this was even worse than before. There was a fundamental problem here that I could not quite put my finger on. The spelling was faultless but for some reason my masterplan had backfired. In the current idiom, my thinking had been fatally flawed.

76

Gradually, I came to realise what had happened. Michelle must have listened to the tape and entered each and every word into the spellchecker as instructed. Faced with a list of correctly spelt words with diverse meanings, she had invariably chosen the wrong one.

I slumped back in the chair. A short while later, I became aware of the office door opening a few inches and Michelle's face appeared. She was wearing a worried frown. She may have called on the off-chance to find out if I had signed my letters. On the other hand, she may have overheard me shouting 'No....... no....... no.......!!' at the top of my voice, whilst pounding the desk with my clenched fists.

Whatever the reason for her visit, with a supreme effort of my iron will I managed to say, in a quite reasonable voice, 'Michelle, would you be kind enough to fetch that electronic thesaurus?'

Michelle darted out of the room and returned a few seconds later, clutching the wretched object in her hand. I took it from her and laid it carefully on the floor. She looked at me in surprise as I stood on the chair. I decided that I wasn't quite high enough and her jaw dropped as I climbed onto the desk.

She clearly thought that this behaviour was rather eccentric even for a person of my advanced years. (To Michelle, anyone over the age of thirty was past their sell-by date and she no doubt thought I was well over-due for a geriatric ward.)

I took careful aim and jumped off the desk, landing heavily on the spelling machine, grinding it into the carpet with my heel.

'GLOBES' flickered briefly on the screen before fading out for ever.

'Thank you, Michelle,' I said. 'That will be all for now.'

She quickly ran to the door with a wide-eyed expression on her face and turned as I called, 'Oh, just pop over to the newsagent's and get a new dictionary, would you?'

CHAPTER 11

FUR CONES

My eldest daughter and another seventeen year old arranged their first holiday without the rest of the family and decided to go to the Costa del Sol. Like most parents, we were rather concerned but knew that the apron-strings had to be cut at some time. Being very independent, they made all their own arrangements and, although feeling rather redundant, I have to admit to a certain amount of grudging admiration.

The girls had to be at Gatwick by 8pm one evening and would be returning at 3am a week later. My wife and I decided that one of us would take them to the airport and the other would collect them. No prizes are being offered for anyone guessing who drew the short straw. I left home at about 1am in a southerly direction, wondering whether I would see them again. Had they been in trouble with the police? Had they been kidnapped by white slave traders? Had they lost their money/passports/tickets? These, and many other worrying questions, crossed my mind.

Since I was a bit early, I stopped on the M25 for a cup of coffee at Clacket Lane Service Area. I then decided to stretch my legs and have a look around the shops. I paused to look into a glass display case containing photographs and pieces of pottery. I was most interested to see that they dated back to Roman times (the pottery, not the photographs).

I went back to the car and continued my journey. Since it was the middle of the night, there was very little traffic about and I soon found a parking space and made my way to the Arrivals lounge. A t.v monitor informed me that the flight would be late and I slumped down into a nearby seat where I could keep an eye on it.

Although there is an excellent range of shops at Gatwick, nothing was open at that time of night apart from the coffee bar and I soon became quite bored. Having not much else to do, my mind wandered and I found myself wondering about the ancient relics in the glass case at the service station. Who had Clacket been? Where was his lane now? As I sat there half awake, it all gradually became perfectly clear to me.......

Shortly after the fast food restaurant at Clacket Lane had opened, a mini bus from a Dartford primary school had arrived during an educational trip in order that its occupants could use the toilet facilities.

A teacher, Mr. David (call me Dave, kids...... please) Ramsbottom and his class of six year old customers, as he had taken to calling them, congregated outside afterwards. They sat and ate their sandwiches in the picnic area.

Little Kylie Biggs amused herself by listening to a tape of her favourite band, 'Kop This!' on her personal stereo. Noticing that she appeared to be enjoying herself, one of her class-mates, Shaun Smith, could not resist making derogatory comments about her choice of music. She had retaliated by attacking him with the nearest object to hand, which happened to be a piece of old flower pot.

Mr. Ramsbottom, noticing what was happening just in time, persuaded Kylie to hand over the weapon. He was about to encourage a group discussion on the unsocial aspects of shoving foreign bodies into peoples ears, when he noticed that it was not a piece of flower pot after all.

Realising that it could be an important find, he forgot all about the lecture he had been about to deliver and put the object into his pocket. On returning home, Mr. Ramsbottom showed the relic to a colleague, who was an amateur historian. The friend became very excited and reported the matter to the appropriate authorities.

Shortly afterwards, the site had been invaded by a group of archaeologists lead by a Professor Spong. The archaeologists had confirmed that the find was a piece of Roman pottery and hoped to discover more. They were not disappointed; having roped off the picnic area where the piece had been found, they spent many weeks carefully digging over the site and sifting through layers of soil.

They succeeded in unearthing hundreds of fragments of pottery ranging in colour from terracotta to off-white. A further twelve months expired whilst the team, under Professor Spong's guidance, painstakingly pieced the fragments together like a three dimensional jigsaw puzzle.

Finally, the professor was ready to make an important announcement. He arranged a Press conference and invited prominent journalists from the world's media to attend.

Professor Spong sat behind a long table on a dais, flanked by his colleagues who looked suitably excited by the enormity of the occasion and eagerly anticipated the reaction to their leader's announcement.

Immediately in front of the Professor, a cloth-covered object stood on the table; in spite of themselves, the world-weary journalists were intrigued and wondered what was hidden there.

The Professor stood up and an expectant hush fell over the assembled gathering. His voice choking with emotion he informed all present that his team of dedicated workers had made a discovery of immense interest not only to historians everywhere, but also to the public at large. He could now prove beyond any shadow of a doubt that the M25 had, by an amazing coincidence, been built on the site of the original Londinium orbital chariot track constructed nearly two thousand years ago.

After all these months, and with the aid of several tubes of superglue, he and his colleagues had pieced together hundreds of pieces of pottery.

He took hold of a corner of the cloth and, with a theatrical flourish, whipped it off to reveal an object resembling a very large inverted ice-cream cornet. The off-white stripe around the middle gave the game away; they had re-constructed the earliest traffic cone known to Mankind. From the thousands of similar fragments left over, Professor Spong and his team had reached the inescapable conclusion that there had been a long line of identical cones along what had once been the XXV(M).

A spontaneous burst of applause came from the audience, before there was a stampede to the nearest telephones.

The Prime Minister appeared on t.v the same evening and was interviewed by a well known presenter. The P.M. was delighted. Here, at last, was a piece of good news. Britain was leading the way again and had clearly done so nearly two thousand years ago when the XXV (M) had been constructed.

The presenter was puzzled.

'Surely, the Romans and not the British were responsible for building roads throughout the land?'

'Nonsense,' responded the P.M. 'Every schoolboy knows that the Romans only built straight roads. Therefore the XXV(M) orbital relief chariot track must have been built using British technology under the supervision of a Briton named Clacket.'

'Can we be certain that Clacket was, in fact, British?' asked the presenter.

Of course we can,' retorted the P.M. 'Whoever heard of a Roman with a name like Clacket? Can you imagine Shakespeare writing "Julius Clacket" or Derek Jacobi playing the title role in a BBC production of "I, Clacket" by Robert Graves? No, or course you can't. Clacket was British, mark my words, and that road was built using good old British know-how.'

The following day the newspapers were full of it. The right-wing papers acclaimed the discovery as being a triumph for the Prime Minister as if he had been personally responsible.

One of the tabloids had the headline 'FUR CONES' on the front page. Displaying its customary disregard for facts, historical or otherwise, there was a brief report, below which there was a cartoon caveman wearing animal skins. He was standing in a chariot with a small dinosaur between the traces. They were stationary behind a line of similar vehicles, flanked on either side by primitive traffic cones. He was shouting 'YABBA-DABBA-DON'T' in frustration. The newspaper speculated upon whether this may have been the first case of something they called 'woad wage.'

I was roused by a kick on the ankle, accompanied by the words, 'Dad, I'm starving.' Apparently, the diet of paella and chips had not been to their liking.

We returned to Clacket Lane where the girls enjoyed a hearty breakfast. I'm quite sure it was delicious but, since it was still only four forty five in the morning, I really couldn't face it and just had a black coffee before setting off home.

CHAPTER 12

THIS WEEK'S BARGAIN

Coming home from Gatwick, there was little traffic on the roads in the early hours of Thursday morning and we arrived at the house shortly after 6.30. I went off to bed for a few hours before going into the office.

I arrived at the office later that morning and was somewhat surprised to find the place a hive of activity. Apparently, we were being inundated with an unprecedented number of enquiries to our advertisement in the local weekly newspaper. Normally, we get one or two enquiries if we are lucky, but today all telephones were ringing at once and the staff were doing their best to cope.

I picked up one of the phones in the reception area. The caller told me that he was a Mr. Jones and he wanted more details concerning a property we were advertising in this week's paper.

'Certainly, Mr. Jones,' I said. 'Which property are you interested in?'

'It's the six bedroom Georgian house with five acres and a heated swimming pool at £24,000,' he replied.

'I'm sorry,' I said, 'but I think you'll find that the property is priced at £375,000.'

'No,' he insisted. 'It definitely says £24,000 here and I want the details sent to me today, first class.'

Still feeling rather bleary-eyed from lack of sleep after my nocturnal visit to the airport, I was in no mood for this type of conversation.

'I inspect every property personally,' I told him rather

pompously. 'I assure you that the house is on the market at £375,000.'

'You can assure me until you are blue in the face, squire,' he snapped. 'It's in the paper so it must be right! Don't bother about the post, I'll call in for the details this afternoon.' With that he put the phone down.

Still feeling that Mr. Jones may have got hold of an old copy of the newspaper, probably circa 1949, I went in search of this week's copy. I quickly thumbed through it until I came to our advertisement. The first thing I noticed was the one bedroom studio flat for sale at £375,000. 'Not many replies to that, I'll be bound,' I muttered grimly to myself, as I realised what had happened. The local rag had made a complete globes-up again, having put the photographs with the wrong captions. You'd think that whoever was responsible would realise that something was amiss; maybe they do. They probably get it right most of the time but can't prevent the odd mistake slipping though.

Whatever the situation, we always get lots of enquiries from hopeful would-be buyers and the more unlikely the advertisement, the bigger the response. I suppose there is some consolation in that it proves that people actually read our advertisement and it is therefore not the total waste of money we sometimes believe it to be.

Since the advent of the Property Misdescriptions Act we always take the precaution of photocopying the advertising copy complete with photographs, before sending it off to the newspaper offices. One cannot be too careful. Someone disappointed at not being able to buy a £375,000 house for £24,000 could complain to the Trading Standards Office and one of their officials could decide to prosecute us; the newspaper would not be held responsible.

The staff had already realised that an error had occurred in the advert and were doing their best to pacify irate callers who were demanding details of the cut-price Georgian house. I left them to it and went into the office to see if any correspondence needed my attention.

Cindy had dealt with most of the post in her usual efficient manner but had left one letter for me to handle personally. It was headed 'KEVIN'S KAR KONSORTIUM' and had an address in Balham, South London. The proprietor, Kevin King, informed me that his Aunt Mavis had died, leaving her property to him.

The solicitor involved, Mr. Krunn of Messrs. Krunn, Krunn, Spottiswood & Krunn required a valuation of the bungalow for Probate purposes, after which it was to be put on the market for sale. It appeared that Aunt Mavis had lived in Battersea for most of her life and had retired to Suffolk some fifteen years earlier. Kevin had not seen her since she had left London, although he had attended the funeral back in Battersea three days ago and now enclosed a front door key.

The property was in a popular part of the town and I went to inspect it. Although the neighbouring properties were well kept, with neat gardens surrounding them, this particular bungalow was looking very forlorn and uncared for. Paint was flaking off the woodwork, the windows were filthy and the once immaculate lawns were knee-deep in weeds.

I put the key in the lock, opened the front door and took an involuntary backward step. The stench was overpowering.

In one split second, I deduced that Aunt Mavis had been partial to fried egg and chips, washed down with quantities of stout and that she had been incontinent. If Sherlock Holmes had been with me, he would no doubt have added that she had once owned a pet rat which had escaped some six months earlier. He would have then proceeded to inform me that the said rat had expired behind the skirting boards due to passively smoking the eighty Turkish cigarettes consumed daily by his mistress.

I hesitated.

I had a clear duty to enter the premises. Not only that, there was a small fee to be earned.

I took a deep breath and plunged in, pausing only to wedge the front door open with a mat. I dashed into the kitchen, ignoring the piles of dirty crockery and rotting vegetables, unbolted the back door and propped it open with a chair. I rushed back down the hall and into the front garden where I exhaled and stood panting from the exertion for a few moments.

I then went and sat in the car for fifteen minutes while the breeze wafted through the bungalow. As soon as I had judged that the smell should have been reduced to merely appaling, I went back inside. I took notes and room measurements in record time and returned to the office feeling decidedly unwell.

I telephoned Kevin who turned out to be a bombastic know-all who had lived in London all his life and had rarely left the capital. He was deeply suspicious of anyone or anything beyond the M25 and was vaguely aware that London was surrounded by somewhere called 'The Country' through which it was necessary to travel in order to get to the 'The Seaside,' which he had visited in his boyhood. He had never been to see Aunt Mavis but knew that Suffolk was somewhere beyond Luton airport.

I gave him my verbal report and valuation which he told me was ridiculously low. In view of his rather insular outlook on life, I wondered how he had managed to form an opinion. It transpired that his assessment owed more to hope than to reality since he had plans to expand his business on the proceeds. I told him I felt my figure was reasonably accurate but he was welcome to try another firm if he felt so inclined. Since I had already mentioned to him that I had grown up in London and knew his area quite well, he felt a bit more inclined to trust my judgement.

He reluctantly agreed that I possibly knew more about the value of his late Aunt's property than he did and asked how much the price would go up if he had central heating and double glazing installed. I wondered, not for the first time in these circumstances, why he had not seen fit to have improvements carried out whilst the old lady had still been alive. I could only conclude that greed had now taken over from indifference. I told him he would be lucky if the value increased by the cost of having these improvements carried out and he said he wouldn't bother.

I told Kevin that I would send my report to the solicitors and would await instructions.

He said he wanted the property sold as fast as possible and rang off.

Whilst all this had been going on, Cindy and Michelle had dealt with thirty five telephone enquiries and six callers in reception concerning the £24,000 Georgian house. All had suspected that a mis-print had occurred but had still made contact 'just in case.' No doubt they were the sort of people who are eternal optimists and find it inconceivable that they didn't match six numbers out of a mere forty nine in the first week of the National Lottery.

During a lull in the afternoon, I telephoned the local newspaper to complain about the mistakes in the advert and demanded a discount. This would be a help but would not compensate for the disruption. I was told that the Manager was busy but would ring back. I signed a batch of letters and went home.

Small independent estate agents like mine need to give a good quality personal service in order to survive, and that frequently means meeting clients outside office hours. Cindy had therefore arranged for me to see a house at seven o'clock that evening as the owners required a valuation.

I understood from her note that the Husband and Wife both worked all day and would be unable to see me any earlier. Having nothing better to do that particular evening, I was happy to comply and hoped that I would come away with definite instructions to sell the property.

I arrived at the house ten minutes early and rang the bell. The door was eventually opened by the householder. I showed him my business card and he rushed back into the living room beckoning me to follow him.

The owner settled himself back in the armchair where he sat with his eyes rivetted to the gigantic television set in the corner which was dominating the room. He, and the rest of the family, which comprised his wife and three children, were engrossed in a programme featuring amateur video clips sent in by members of the public. These snippets of video tape seemed to consist largely of people falling over, and were the source of much amusement.

Someone gestured towards another chair but I was anxious to get on with my job rather than joining them in watching this banal programme. Besides, I didn't want to be too late home and miss the beginning of Coronation Street.

My opening gambit was, as usual, to ask why the family was considering moving. Was there a new job in the offing? Did they need a larger or smaller property? This established at the outset whether or not I was wasting my time. It was not unknown for someone to ask me out on a wild goose chase simply because he was curious to know whether it had gone up or down in value. I am always suspicious when people then demand that I put my valuation in writing. I am inclined to suspect that they have no intention of moving and need a written valuation for some other purpose and are trying to avoid paying the normal fee.

However, I digress. The owner shot an irritated glance in my direction and held up his hand. Keeping his eyes glued to the t.v, he said,

'Hang on a minute, mate, it's nearly finished.'

I took this to mean the show he was watching and realised why he had made the appointment for seven o'clock. He hadn't wanted to miss his programme and by arriving ten minutes early, I had deprived him of thirty seconds of this entertainment whilst he was answering the doorbell.

'Is it all right if I have a look round?' I whispered.

'Help yourself, mate,' he replied, continuing to stare at the box.

I wandered around the house taking notes and measurements of the rooms. I listed carpets, curtains, kitchen appliances etc. separately so that I could check whether or not the owners intended leaving them, just as soon as I was allowed to speak.

When I returned to the living room, the owner indicated an armchair and I sat down. The programme had reached its climax.

The star feature of the evening was a clip showing a man working at a sausage making machine in a food processing factory. Unsurprisingly, he fell in and emerged at the other end as twelve stone of chipolatas neatly divided up into one hundred and sixty eight one pound cellophane-wrapped packages. Luckily, his best friend and workmate had happened to have his camcorder with him and was able to record the event for posterity, send in the tape and claim the five hundred pounds star prize for the winning entry.

The hilarity of the studio audience knew no bounds; there were hoots of laughter, much shoulder shaking and thigh slapping. The host was grinning happily and informing the viewers that they, and not he, were the stars of the show. He implored them to keep their favourite video clips rolling in.

As the advertisements came on, the husband and wife reluctantly turned their attention to me and fractionally turned the sound down. The children continued staring at the television set.

'Where are you thinking of moving to?' I asked, somewhat ungrammatically.

'Well, we're running a bit short of space,' the husband replied. 'The kids are growing up. Two of them are sharing a bedroom at the moment and we need an extra one. There's always fights about which programme to watch; they can each have their own telly then.'

Whatever happened to playing games? I wondered. When I was their age I would have been out in the garden playing cowboys and native Americans, not spending all my leisure time watching t.v. However, it was none of my business.

I told them my opinion of the value and we agreed upon the asking price, which was slightly higher, since purchasers invariably believed that owners would be open to offers. They then signed my 'terms of business' form agreeing to leave the property with me as their sole agent for a period of eight weeks. It is now fairly common practice for estate agents to use these forms.

I cannot speak for anyone else, but I find they are a useful defence against unscrupulous agents of the Floggitt & Quick variety. Estate Agents spend a considerable amount of money in marketing a property and it is therefore rather galling to have it poached by a predatory agent who keeps pestering the owner for instructions until they finally give way and let him have it. The reason I erect 'for sale' boards is to attract buyers and not these parasites!

I told my new clients that I would return next morning in order to erect the board and take photographs. I warned them that when they got home that evening, they would no doubt find two or three business cards from other agents on the doormat. It was also possible that they would find a letter from Floggit & Quick, addressed to them personally, purporting to have a 'Mr. X' who would 'definitely' want to buy their house, given the chance. I informed them that if 'Mr. X' existed outside Flogitt & Quick's fertile imagination, he would almost certainly be on my mailing list as well as theirs and would automatically be sent particulars.

By this time, the commercial break had finished and the next programme was about to start. Realising that further attempts at conversation were doomed to failure, I bade them farewell and let myself out.

CHAPTER 13

AFTERNOON TEE

The Yookay Building Society's golf tournament day had arrived at last. I was looking forward to it. I don't know why since my game is usually more reminiscent of hockey than it is golf. I think they ought to change the rules and make the winner the person who hits the ball more often than anyone else.

The competition was at a course about ten miles away and did not start until two p.m. I therefore had plenty of time to dictate some letters, deal with a few telephone calls and carry out a valuation.

My first task, after dictating a tape and giving it to Cindy, was to go back to the house I had seen the night before. I took my usual anti-Flogitt & Quick route and arrived at the property without mishap. I put up the 'for sale' board, took a photograph and went on to my next appointment.

The owners of the bungalow had come in the previous afternoon and told me that they wanted to put it on the market. The man told me that the name of their property was 'Withanee' in London Road and that their name was Clarke.

'Is that........,' I'd begun, and then realised why he had given his property such an unusual name. 'Mr. & Mrs. Clarke, "Withanee", London Road,' I had written in my diary.

It was only half a mile from my previous call and I soon arrived. I slowed down when approaching the property, checked all my mirrors and made sure that I was not being followed. The coast was clear and I parked the car outside a property twenty yards away. (I did not believe in being too careful).

I walked up the garden path, automatically noting the neatly trimmed lawns, clematis climbing up the porch and the standard rose bushes.

I rang the bell; it played the theme from 'Love Story.' I waited for Mr. & Mrs. Clarke to come to the door and pictured the interior: thick pile carpets, Laura Ashley wallpaper everywhere and a knitted poodle disguising the spare loo roll in the bathroom.

'Ah, come in,' Mrs. Clarke said.

I was ushered into the lounge and she kindly went off to make some tea.

Mr. Clarke put his Daily Telegraph crossword puzzle away and told me that the garden was now too big for them and that they were contemplating moving into a sheltered flat in a warden-controlled development reserved for the over fifty fives. They therefore wanted to put their bungalow on the market immediately.

Mr. Clarke returned with tea and biscuits. She and her husband were a very pleasant couple and the type of people I particularly liked dealing with; straightforward, appreciative of the type of service we try to offer and unlikely to be influenced by the likes of Flogitt & Quick. They had occupied the property since they had retired ten years earlier and were now ready to move on.

'I've got the other agent's particulars from when we bought it,' Mrs. Clarke told me helpfully. 'It will save some time.'

'That's very thoughtful of you,' I said, 'but I'd rather take my own notes and room measurements, thanks all the same.'

'I think they're all right,' Mr. Clarke added.

'I expect they are,' I said, 'but since the Property Misdescriptions Act came into force, we have to be extremely careful. If I copy another agent's error from ten years ago, I could be sued. If I'm careless enough to make a mistake, it'll be my own fault.'

'Well, I suppose estate agents only have themselves to blame,' Mr Clarke said. 'All that exaggeration some of you go in for. It's a pity you can't all be more like that agent who used to put the funny adverts in the Sunday papers. He used to tell the truth.'

It's amazing how many people remember the late Roy Brooks, who ran a successful estate agency in London, and his unique style of advertising, although they never seem to recall his name. I well remember the pleasure of reading his witty advertisements in the 1960s and early 70s although I'm not sure whether 'truth' had much to do with them. He had the Trendies of the time queuing up from Chelsea to Hampstead to have themselves and their homes insulted in the nicest possible way.

Regrettably, Roy Brooks had died in the early 1970s and his advertising style has been attempted several times since but, as far as I am aware, never equalled. Thanks to the Property Misdescriptions Act it now never will be; God only knows what Roy Brooks would have made of it all.

I decided to test a theory.

'You've moved quite a few times, Mr. Clarke,' I said. 'How many grossly inaccurate estate agents' particulars have you come across?'

He thought for a moment.

'I can't remember off-hand,' he said, 'but you're all well known for your flowery language; and your attempts to make a silk purse out of a sow's ear,' he added with a smile.

'We get a lot of sow's ears,' I agreed, 'but there's a difference between trying to extol the virtues of a property in order to sell it, and quite another to tell outright lies about it. I've been in the business a very long time and I can honestly say I have never come across the latter.'

He looked at me doubtfully.

'I can assure you that's true,' I insisted. 'We've all seen magazine articles with prime examples of excerpts from outrageous house particulars. I'm not saying they were not authentic, but I've certainly never seen any. I'm inclined to think they're made up by journalists desperate to beat a deadline,' I added, borrowing one of Frank's theories.

Mr. & Mrs. Clarke exchanged glances. They obviously thought I was paranoid about it and maybe they were right! They quickly changed the subject and showed me over their property. I discovered that the wallpaper throughout was by Laura Ashley, as I had anticipated, but that the spare loo roll was hidden under the skirts of a flamenco dancer.

I said goodbye, took photographs of the property and returned to the office. Several messages awaited my return and I spent the next half hour on the telephone.

The local vicar had called whilst I was out and I rang him back. Having an unusual name myself, I am quite interested in other people's names but had never come across anyone called 'Emm' before. I resolved to ask him, when we met, whether he knew the origin of his name. His wife put me on 'hold' while she went to get him from the garden. I sat there involuntarily listening to an electronic version of 'Onward Christian Soldiers' whilst I waited for him to come on to the line.

The Rev. Ronald Emm told me that he was looking for a bungalow for his forthcoming retirement and wanted my personal attention. I told him that I had just seen exactly what he was looking for and arranged for him to view Mr. & Mrs. Clarke's property. I was convinced that he would buy it and, if so, it would have been a very easy sale. This sort of think happens occasionally and tends to make up for the 9, Mafeking Terraces of this world.

Towards the end of the morning, the advertising manager of the local paper telephoned as I was on the way out of the front door. Cindy told her that I was about to commit G.B.H. on a little white ball and would telephone her back the following day.

I went straight to the car-park, making no attempt at secrecy. I was gratified to note in my rear view mirror that

Daryl happened to be limping towards his car. I drove out of the car park and as soon as I was well beyond the invisible boundary of my normal territory, he drove completely around a roundabout and headed back the way he had come. It gave me considerable satisfaction to know that he had wasted his time and petrol.

I arrived at the Golf Club at lunchtime and went to the bar where entrants for the competition were meeting, to find out what time I would be playing.

I went up to a group of people I knew and one of them offered to buy me a pint. I politely refused, saying that I found golf a difficult enough game as it was without making it worse for myself by imbibing alcohol. I reminded him of the well-known slogan, 'If you drink, don't drive, pitch or putt,' and settled for a soft drink instead.

I checked the list of entrants and went off to find the three people I would be playing with. Three and a half hours and a particularly unremarkable round later, I wondered whether my score might have been better after all if I'd had a pint or two beforehand. I threw my clubs into the boot of the car in disgust and went back to the club-house.

There was a buzz of conversation in the changing rooms after the match, although 'conversation' is perhaps a rather misleading term since everyone was talking at once and no-one was listening. As usual, everybody had their own tales to tell, their triumphs and disasters, the good luck and the bad.

Someone handed me a drink and started spouting forth:

'I was standing on the fourth tee with a three iron in my hand....... No, I tell a lie. It was the third tee and I hit a four iron....... As you were. It was definitely the fourth tee and I drove off with a three wood. Or was it a driver? Anyway....... '

He sensed someone else coming towards him and turned to include them in the 'conversation.' I took the opportunity to make good my escape but there was none; everyone else was engrossed in his own personal monologue. I therefore joined the ritual, but no-one listened to me either. Having washed and changed, we trooped through to the bar and continued boring each other to death by dissecting our game and re-living every stroke until the signal was given that dinner was about to be served.

We wended our way into the dining room and I found myself sitting next to an old acquaintance who looked rather glum.

'Cheer up,' Eric, I said. 'It may never happen.' (I'm full of original comments like that).

'It already has,' he replied with equal originality. 'Old Cyril should have been here today. You remember Cyril - he was my playing partner for thirty years. Died two weeks ago.'

I paused with a spoonful of the inevitable prawn cocktail half-way to my mouth.

'That's terrible,' I said. 'What happened?'

'Well,' Eric said, 'he went the way he would have wanted to go; on the golf course. We were playing our regular Friday afternoon round.......'

His voice faltered as he tried to control his emotions. I poured some water into a glass for him and, after a few moments, he was able to continue.

'We were standing on the eighteenth green. The score couldn't have been closer. Cyril was very nervous but putted first and managed to sink the ball in the hole. I needed to putt mine from four feet to win by one stroke.'

He paused again to take a sip of water. He managed to continue, his voice choking with emotion.

'Cyril picked his ball out of the hole, walked back towards me and suddenly collapsed. Fell right on top of my ball. Dead before he hit the ground!'

'How dreadful!' I exclaimed. 'Whatever did you do?'

He pushed his steak and kidney pie away, quite unable to finish it.

'Well, I didn't know quite what to do really,' he said. 'I

felt for a pulse but there wasn't one. I tried moving him but he was a big man. Must have been sixteen stone.'

He paused while the waiter cleared away the plates and poured out the coffee.

'In the end, I just had to drop another ball as close as I could to the original one and putt out from there,' he said.

'So you managed to win the game, then?' I commented. 'The afternoon wasn't a total disaster.'

'You haven't heard the whole story, yet!' he blurted out.' I went directly over to the club house and reported the matter to the secretary. He said I should have told him as soon as it had happened.'

I frowned.

'You couldn't have told him much sooner, surely?' I said.

'He said that if he'd known what had happened he would have sent two greenkeepers over and they would have moved the body without disturbing the ball. You'll never believe what he did next!'

He had my undivided attention.

'Go on, surprise me!' I said.

'He only took my scorecard and deducted two penalty strokes for playing the wrong ball!'

'The unfeeling swine!' I exclaimed. 'So instead of winning by one stroke, you lost by one! Just the sort of thing he would do, arrogant blighter.'

I suddenly had an idea.

'Why don't you write to the Royal and Ancient Golf Club in St. Andrews and get a ruling from them?' I suggested. 'They're the people who make up the rules and I don't think there's anything that covers that situation.'

He brightened up a bit.

'Do you really think I should?' he asked.

'Definitely,' I said. 'They're bound to over-rule him. Anyway, Cyril wouldn't have wanted to win that way. He was a real sportsman. By the way, did you manage to get along to the funeral?'

'Yes,' he said. 'Luckily it was on the same afternoon as

the monthly Ladies match so I was able to go. As a matter of fact, I represented his widow since she was playing in the match.'

We both spoke at once. 'It was what Cyril would have wanted,' we agreed.

There was a rapping noise from the top table. The club captain was banging a spoon on the table to gain everyone's attention before announcing the prize winners. He began giving a rambling speech, thanking everyone concerned with making the day a success. This was the point were I started losing interest. My rather pathetic scorecard was unlikely to merit much attention. I opened one eye when he mentioned the 'nearest the pin' prize winner. This is the person who gets his ball closest to the hole on a nominated green from his first shot off the tee. Rather unusually the winner in this case was Basil who had scored a hole-in-one. I already knew that since he had been my playing partner.

Basil went up to collect his prize and made a rather smug speech brimming with false modesty, saying that he was really delighted to have scored his first 'ace' after so many years of playing. I admired his cheek since I recalled what had actually happened.

Basil had stood on the tee eyeing up the flagstick some 150 yards away. Carefully placing his ball in position, he had then tossed a handful of dried grass into the air to assess the wind direction. Since there was a gale blowing from behind, I don't know why he had bothered, but I suppose it was something he had picked up from watching the professionals on the telly.

Basil had taken one last look at the green and then taken an almighty swipe at the ball. It was one of those rare occasions when he had managed to hit it dead centre with a near-perfect swing Nick Faldo would have been delighted with and the ball had responded by flying off down the fairway like a bat out of hell.

Unfortunately, he had not only wildly over-estimated the distance to the green but had also been aiming at least twenty yards too far to the right. Aided by the gale-force wind, the ball should have ended up deep in the woods, buried under three feet of leaf-mould never to been seen again, had its flight not been impeded.

As luck would have it, however, the ball had ricocheted off a conveniently placed oak tree and skidded through a bunker, alarming a pigeon which had been foraging for insects nearby. The startled bird had fluttered into the air and flapped around the green in a blind panic. Having lost most of its momentum, the ball had rolled sedately across the green and come to rest on the very brink of the hole.

By coincidence, the pigeon was impelled to answer a call of nature when it happened to be directly over the hole. It scored a direct hit on the side of the ball, causing it to topple in .

Observing the unexpected disappearance of the ball, Basil had sprinted down the fairway, whooping with delight, fished it out of the hole and, pausing briefly to wipe it clean on the grass, held it triumphantly aloft. This rather un-British behaviour had been bad enough, but when he had had the nerve to stand there accepting everyones' congratulations, along with his prize, I cringed with embarrassment.

I felt my eyes start to glaze over again while other prize winners collected their trophies. I gradually became aware that someone was calling my name. Eric gave me a nudge. No, I was not dreaming, I had actually won a prize!

I got to my feet, squeezed past the chairs and came before the captain. He shook my hand and handed over the prize, which just happened to be a book about golf. He congratulated me on achieving the award for 'Busiest Golfer of the Afternoon.' Still feeling somewhat bewildered by this turn of events, I thanked him and returned to my seat.

I felt rather pleased with myself. 'Busiest Golfer,' eh? I gradually realised the significance of the award. The general idea of the game is to strike the ball the least possible number of times between the first tee and the eighteenth hole. However, I had actually hit it more often than anyone else that afternoon, hence I had the honour of receiving recognition as being the 'Busiest Golfer of the afternoon.' In other words, it was the booby prize.

I examined the book. It was entitled, 'Ten Easy Ways To Improve Your Golf.'

CHAPTER 14

On the buses

I arrived bright and early at the office the following day, opened the post and checked the messages left for me. I was delighted to see that the Rev. Emm had agreed to buy 'Withanee,' had the cash available and wanted to complete the deal in record time. I wondered whether he would change the name when he retired there. It could be rather confusing if he didn't. Perhaps he would christen it 'Dunpreachin'' or something similar.

Cindy had dealt with the negotiations in her usual ultra-efficient manner and had sent the relevant information off to the solicitors, who would then prepare the draft contract. The first telephone call of the day was from my accountant.

'I've got good news and I've got bad news,' he announced.

'All right, let's have the good news first,' I said.

'Right. You won't have any V.A.T to pay this quarter.'

'Excellent,' I said. 'I knew I could rely on you to look after my interests. What's the bad news?'

He hesitated.

'Um, I'm afraid your income for the period was extremely low and your outgoings were exceptionally high. Therefore, you won't have to pay anything to Customs and Excise.'

'Well done!' I said. 'You're worth every penny I pay you and I'm going to recommend you to my friends.'

'Um, that's another thing I was going to mention,' he said. 'You haven't actually settled any of my bills over the last two years.'

I gave the matter a few moments thought and came up with a brilliant idea.

'Here's what I'm going to do,' I told him. 'I'll have the shop fitters come in and build a new fascia on the office, throw out all the existing furniture and have it replaced with new, have all my "for sale" boards re-designed and replaced and have an extra page of advertising in the local rag each week!'

There was a stunned silence from the other end.

He finally managed to stammer, 'How's that going to help?'

I carefully explained it to him as though I was speaking to a somewhat retarded seven year old.

'It's fairly obvious I should have thought,' I said. 'At the end of the next quarter, provided we don't sell too many houses, Customs and Excise will owe me a considerable sum of money. I will then pay you out of that.'

Cindy put her head around the door and told me she had a call waiting.

'But......,' began the accountant.

'Sorry,' I said. 'Duty calls. I'll be in touch,' and I put the phone down.

Cindy put the caller through. It was only Frank Lee. However, he wasn't ringing to discuss his strange malady, he wanted to do some business. He had been approached by a client who wanted to sell a large country house between our two towns. The client wanted it offered for sale from my town as well as Frank's and since Far & Wide did not have a branch office here, Frank had suggested a joint sole agency with my firm. An appointment had been made to inspect 23, Meadowview Lane in the afternoon and I suggested that we met at our usual hostelry at lunchtime.

I was interested to note that Cheddargorgers' lunch was still listed on the 'chalkboard' and assumed that no bricks had been thrown through the windows by militant activists.

I settled for the wild mushrooms on toast and wondered if

they tasted any different from the tame ones I usually bought in Tesco's. Frank just had a packet of Ginseng flavoured crisps.

'What's the problem now?' I asked him, noticing he was rather down in the dumps.

'Well, he's getting worst than ever,' complained Frank. 'I can't understand what he's talking about. I must be getting old.'

I didn't need to ask who he was referring to; I knew it was fatal to encourage him, but luckily had an hour to spare and settled myself back in the fireside chair.

Frank went on to tell me about the regular Wednesday afternoon meeting he had attended at Head Office. He particularly remembered it had been Wednesday, since it had been the last day of the month and he had spent the entire morning compiling statistics for his 'end of month' report for Head Office. El Cid had been in the Chair as usual and had presided over the meeting in his own inimitable style.

'I'm not sure that all of you are up to speed with the focus of our management structure,' El Cid had said, somewhat bafflingly. 'I have now been promoted to assistant to the Assistant Chief Executive and my duties have been subject to augmentation alignment with particular control over creative budgeting. Following the success of our rationalisation programme.......'

Frank felt it was time for clarification and interrupted.

'Do you mean the office shut-downs?' he asked.

L.C. ignored him and carried on, emphasising the first sentence and glaring at Frank.

'Following the success of our rationalisation programme,' he repeated, 'we have had an excellent year in which an overall negative profit of five million pounds below last year's has been achieved.'

He paused for dramatic effect and beamed at the staff assembled in front of him. His pleasure was short-lived as Frank again sought enlightenment.

'Does that mean we only lost six million quid compared with eleven million last year?' he enquired.

The effect could not have been more dramatic if he had entered Westminster Abbey during a state funeral and shouted a stream of foul obscenities at the top of his voice. L.C. went purple in the face and was incapable of coherent speech; Frank wondered if he was about to witness an authentic case of spontaneous human combustion.

When he was finally able to speak, L.C. told Frank that he was never, ever, to mention the word 'loss' again and that he would live to regret the consequences if he did.

Frank went on to tell me that the firm was continuing to be worried about the Property Misdescriptions Act and it was emphasised again and again that everyone should exercise 'all due diligence.' The problem was that they were going to ludicrous lengths to comply with that well worn phrase.

Time was getting on and, having finished our lunch, I set off for the property with Frank following on behind in his own car. We pulled up at the house and I was concerned to see that Frank's face had turned ashen.

'What's the matter?' I asked. 'Are you ill?'

He lifted up a trembling hand and I followed the direction of his pointing finger.

'I'm not putting that in my particulars,' he said. 'No way!'

He was indicating the name of the house which was attached to the gate. 'Shangri-la,' it proclaimed to the world.

'The owner may consider this place to be a paradise,' he went on. 'You and I might agree with him that it's heaven on earth, but what about the Skinhead from Hackney Greyhound Stadium?'

I was baffled.

'You've got me beaten,' I told him. 'What Skinhead?'

'Sorry,' he said. 'I was forgetting that you don't go to our training meetings. It's the one Elsie was talking about.'

I was none the wiser and said so.

'It's the archetypal man-in-the-street,' he explained patiently. The average person. The Mr., Mrs., or Ms Anybody. The one we refer to when we're trying to establish what is, or is not, acceptable wording for our particulars.'

I was still puzzled and he continued to elucidate.

'If any of us feels that a statement in our particulars could be misconstrued, we give it what Elsie calls the ultimate litmus test. In other words, we say, "What would the Skinhead from Hackney Greyhound Stadium understand from that statement?"

I was just as bewildered as before.

'I thought that was the "Man on the Clapham Omnibus," I said.

'Well it was,' he admitted, 'but since the buses have been on strike for the past two weeks, we've had to make him redundant. El Cid thought it was rather misleading to mention him when the buses aren't running.'

'But why invent the Skinhead from Hackney Greyhound Stadium?' I asked.

'Well, I think it's all to do with the modern trend of bringing everything down to the lowest possible level,' he told me. 'I said we ought to keep the feminists happy by saying the "Lady of Ill-repute from King's Cross," but Elsie thought I was being facetious.'

Further comment failed me and I suggested that we went inside and met the owner of the property.

Mr. Wellposh was an elegant and successful businessman in his mid forties who had recently been appointed Managing Director of a manufacturing group. He and his wife had decided that they would now need to entertain customers and clients more often and required an even bigger house than the one they owned at present.

Frank and I proceeded to take notes and room measurements for the next hour or so and agreed a suitable asking price with the owner. I told Mr. Wellposh that Frank and I would pool our resources and knowledge of the local market and do our best to find a buyer in the shortest space of time.

We all shook hands and Frank and I returned to my car. We both sat in it for a few minutes to discuss the property and our strategy for trying to sell it.

'We'd better describe it as a detached five bedroom house with garden,' Frank said.

'This is not your ordinary "run-of-the-mill" property,' I reminded him. 'I think we'll need to use a bit more imagination.'

He looked at me warily.

'How do you mean?' he asked.

'I thought perhaps we should say something like, "a delightful gentlemens' residence in immaculate condition standing in two acres of tree-studded park land and enjoying panoramic views over the surrounding countryside," I said.

His jaw dropped.

'Wash your mouth out!' he exclaimed. 'I can't possibly put that.'

'I know, I know,' I said. 'The Skinhead from Hackney Greyhound Stadium wouldn't agree. He'd probably describe it as a load of old ballcocks or words to that effect, but that's how I'm going to describe it. You can do what you like with your own particulars.'

'Well, don't mention my firm's name in any newspaper advert if you do,' he said. 'El Cid will go bananas if he sees it.'

'I really think this Property Misdescriptions nonsense is getting out of hand,' I told him. 'I'm a bit worried about your state of mind. I'm bad enough, but you should consider taking professional advice.'

'You mean see a psychiatrist, I suppose,' he said angrily. 'I'm not barmy, you know. I'm just trying to follow company guidelines.'

With that, we each went our separate ways. On my way back to the office, I couldn't help worrying about Frank. It was bad enough that he was now bothering about what Elsie thought of him but another recent incident convinced me that his condition was getting really serious.

When I had first met Frank some years earlier, I had soon come to realise that he was obsessed with his job and rarely talked about anything else. Also, since his wife had left him, I knew that he now filled in his spare time with some rather peculiar hobbies. However, it had still come as a shock when he'd mentioned in passing that he had amassed 50,000 matchsticks and was now spending his evenings building a scale model of Arbon House in Warwick. I immediately realised that he was in desperate need of help. Psychiatric help that is, not assistance in recreating the headquarters of the National Association of Estate Agents in miniature.

I was going to have to make a point of seeing the doctor on his behalf. It was quite obvious that he wouldn't go himself.

CHAPTER 15

A CONSULTATION

As soon as I arrived back at the office towards the end of the afternoon, I dictated the particulars of 'Shangri-la,' signed a few letters and made some phone calls before setting off home. Normally, I walk to and from home, but since I had been using the car that day, I went to the car park. I switched on the car radio and tuned into Radio 4; a 'chat show' was in progress and the interviewer was talking to a panel of experts about the economy in general and the housing market in particular.

An executive from an insurance company which still owned a diminishing chain of estate agencies, was giving his opinion that the market was improving and that 'negative equity' would become a thing of the past within five years. His firm was, apparently, eagerly looking forward to renewed prosperity in the near future. His opposite number, from a building society, had personally been responsible for his company's undignified scramble to buy up estate agents' offices in the mid 1980s. He had decided to cut his losses eighteen months earlier and, with his colleagues' agreement, had sold off his little empire to whoever would take them off his hands.

The whole sorry episode had lasted for eight years, many millions of pounds had been wasted, offices had been closed down and a large number of staff had lost their jobs. Surprisingly, his own job had not been among them and he still received an exorbitant salary and all the usual perks. He was now saying that he really couldn't see any improvement taking place in the foreseeable future and that people would be well advised to put their money into savings plans rather than into property. Try telling that to first time buyers, I thought.

I continued homewards and, as I parked the car, I happened to see my doctor acquaintance walking past my house. I called out to him. He stopped and we had a brief chat before I brought up the problems that had been bothering me, mainly on Frank's behalf.

'I've got this friend who has a rather worrying problem,' I began.

He looked at me suspiciously.

'Why don't you consult your own doctor?' he asked.

'Well, I don't want to bother him in the surgery,' I said. 'I know how busy you all are, and since you live just down the road and we're neighbours, I thought perhaps we could keep it informal.'

He looked even more wary.

'Look, it's not at all ethical for me to talk to someone else's patient,' he said, 'but since I know you and as you say it's for somebody else, I'm willing to listen but I can't promise anything.'

I thanked him and we walked along the road together towards his house, continuing the conversation as we went.

'If this is a confidential problem,' he said, 'you ought to go along to the clinic. You'll be well looked after there.'

'It's nothing to do with me,' I said. 'It's my friend I'm worried about.'

'Oh yes, so you said,' he muttered.

By this time, we had reached his house and he invited me in. We went into the lounge and as soon as we had sat down, he leaned towards me with a frown on his face and adopted his best bedside manner.

'Look, why can't you just be honest with me. It's you isn't it? You're the one with the problem, aren't you?'

'Well, all right, it's me as well,' I admitted. 'I'm affected to a lesser extent.'

He looked exasperated.

'Look, there's really no need to be coy about this,' he said. 'I'm used to hearing about intimate problems. What are your symptoms? Any nasty rashes? Swellings? Unpleasant discharges?'

'Of course I haven't got any of those symptoms,' I said. 'Whatever made you think I have?'

He looked me steadily in the eye.

'We are talking about a sexually transmitted disease here, aren't we?' he asked.

I was horrified.

'Certainly not!' I said, indignantly. 'Don't you people think about anything else?'

He seemed slightly disappointed.

'Perhaps it would be a good idea if you started again,' he grumbled. 'I'm not a mind reader, you know.'

I explained that, as estate agents, Frank and I were becoming more affected by legislation than ever before and were doing our best to cope with all the new rules and regulations, as they came into force.

He looked particularly unsympathetic.

'It's about time your type of business came under more control,' he commented.

'I couldn't agree more,' I told him. 'Frank and I are just about fed up with the "cowboy" element giving the rest of us a bad name. You may not be aware of it, but organisations such as the National Association of Estate Agents have been advocating better control for years.'

'What's the problem, then?' he asked, becoming interested in spite of himself.

'The problem is the Property Misdescriptions Act,' I told him. 'I'm sure that whoever thought it up had the best of intentions, but the day-to-day interpretation is becoming farcical.'

'How have you and your friend been affected?' he asked.

'Well,' I said, 'for a start, we've had to delete all adjectives from our leaflets, we're no longer allowed to rely on information supplied by clients and even genuine errors are punishable with a hefty fine, not to mention the criminal record that goes with it.'

'That does sound a bit Draconian,' he said, but I can't really imagine the "Powers That Be" wasting too much time on trivial cases. Surely they've got better things to do.'

'You'd certainly think so,' I said, 'but take a case I heard about the other day. An agent told me that a Trading Standards officer inspected his records and the only criticism he could come up with was that a set of particulars stated that the garden was "small."

'I find that hard to believe,' he said. 'Surely, no-one would be that petty?'

'Well, I suppose he may have been joking,' I conceded, 'but he didn't seem to be. Also, we're having trouble with photographs; they're deemed to be stand-alone statements for the purposes of the Act.'

'No bad thing, surely,' he commented.

'Well, as a matter of fact it is making life complicated,' I said. 'Take a hypothetical case: I am selling a bungalow which started life as a pre-fab and later had a brick skin built around the outside.'

He nodded to show that he had the vision firmly in his mind's eye.

'I take a photograph and stick it above the written description I have prepared,' I continued. 'My particulars state quite clearly beneath the photograph that the property is of non-standard construction.'

He carried on nodding sagely.

'However, it doesn't matter that I have put in this qualification; it's too late because the statement, in the form of the photo has already been made.'

He did his best to look as if he was making sense of what I was telling him.

'I am therefore still contravening the Act since the property gives the appearance in the photo of being a conventional modern bungalow.'

111

'That doesn't make any sense,' he said. 'Why are trading standards officers being so vindictive, anyway?'

'I think the difficulty is that they have no option,' I told him. 'They have to follow up any complaint, no matter how frivolous. They don't make laws, they simply apply them. Officials have a much more sensible approach on the Continent towards idiotic rules and regulations; they just ignore them.'

'No wonder you're getting paranoid about it,' he said. 'It seems that a little common sense wouldn't go amiss. You were going to tell me a bit more about how all this has been affecting you.......'

I went on to tell him that, as a result of constantly attempting to comply with the Act, we were accepting everything at face value and were taking every figure of speech literally.

'It's got beyond a joke,' I told him. 'We're forever tying ourselves up in knots.'

'Not literally, I hope,' he smiled.

I was horror-stricken by what I had just said.

'I'm so sorry,' I said, 'I really didn't mean to say that. When I said that we were tied.......'

'Yes, all right, all right,' he said. 'I realise it was only a figure of speech. Look, this case is beginning to interest me. I'll make a few enquiries, off the record, and if I come up with anything, I'll let you know but you really must keep to your own G.P. in future.'

I thanked him for his time and trouble and went home.

CHAPTER 16

A Glimmer of Hope

I left home the following morning, having had to change the blade in my razor yet again; I strongly suspected that someone had used it for sharpening school pencils and had thought that I wouldn't notice.

I arrived at the office to find Cindy and Michelle beaming from ear to ear. Apparently a piece of news they thought would please me had just been relayed to them by a reliable source. According to the shopkeeper next door to Flogitt & Quick, they were in serious trouble, having upset one of their clients, who was about to report them to the Office of Fair Trading.

Flogitt & Quick, like many agents in the area, had frequent dealings with USAF personnel from local air bases who bought, sold and rented properties during their tours of duty. One of the higher ranking officers, Col. Irwin T. Budweisser, Jr., had received sudden orders to return to the States and had put his house up for sale with F & Q. He had left at such short notice that it was still fully furnished and he intended to come back and arrange for everything to be shipped back to Florida when the house was sold.

As soon as he was safely five thousand miles away across the Atlantic, Daryl had discovered a way of earning some easy money. Not having had any success in finding a buyer, he had seen no harm in renting it out to three airmen who had asked him for accommodation.

The Colonel had returned to the local base due to some emergency and had arrived back at his house during the night looking forward to a well-earned sleep. Feeling rather tired and suffering from jet-lag, his temper was not improved when he had found his property occupied by total strangers, sitting around watching his T.V. Since it was well past midnight, the unofficial tenants, being rather bleary-eyed from imbibing the Colonel's beer, did not realise who he was and had the impression that they were being burgled. In the resultant melee, punches were thrown, furniture was smashed and windows were broken before the police arrived, having been summoned by the next door neighbour.

I sat behind my desk and felt a warm glow of satisfaction; perhaps the old adage that 'cheats never prosper' was true after all. I looked forward to hearing the next instalment of this fascinating saga, but had business to attend to in the meantime. I read through the morning's post, discarded the bills until later and dictated suitable replies to the remainder. I then remembered that I had left a jacket at the Dry Cleaners the day before and that it had been promised for today. If I didn't pick it up while it was fresh in my memory, it would probably still be there in six months time.

I walked down the road to the shop and waited behind a lady who was first in the queue. I had business on my mind, as usual and was thinking about the sale of 'Withanee,' which was due to be completed within the next few days. Suddenly, the door burst open and the Rev. Emm arrived on the scene looking wild-eyed and panic-stricken. He had left his car immediately outside the shop on the double yellow lines, engine running.

'Speak of the Devil!' I exclaimed. 'I was just thinking about you!'

'Oh, sorry,' I added, realising what I had just said. 'No offence meant.'

He looked so agitated that he didn't appear to register what I had said. He went straight to the front of the queue.

'I hope you don't mind me pushing in,' he said to nobody

in particular, 'but this is an emergency. I'm officiating at a wedding in three hours time and I must have this cleaned.'

He handed a garment over to the assistant, who reluctantly took it from him. She glanced doubtfully between the other customer and myself.

The Rev. Emm was suitably apologetic.

'I don't know how it happened,' he said, 'but a stray cat got locked in the vestry all night and it's done something revolting on my best cassock.'

The assistant immediately dropped the offending item like a hot potato and wrinkled her nose in disgust.

'Haven't you got another one, then?' she asked.

'Well, yes I have, but it's at home in the wash and we haven't got a tumble drier, so we can't get it ready on time,' he said, becoming more frantic by the minute. 'You must help me,' and added desperately, 'please!'

'I'll see what I can do,' she said, beginning to look quite faint.

'I'd be so grateful,' he said with immense relief. 'It'll be my last wedding before I retire. I'm moving next week.'

'Can I have your name and address, then,?' she asked.

He glanced out of the door at his car, clearly anxious to be on his way.

'Emm, "Withanee," London Road,' he said hurriedly.

She wrote on the ticket and then drew back from it slightly, giving it a sidelong, uncertain look. Being curious, I craned my neck to see what she had written.

The ticket bore the inscription, 'Mr. Me, London Road.'

I decided to be helpful.

'The gentleman's name is "Emm," I said.

An expression of awestruck awareness crossed her face.

''ere,' she said, 'was you in them old James Bond films?'

'No I was not in them, those, old James Bond films,' he snapped impatiently. 'My name is "Emm"....... Ronald Emm. That's capital "E," double "m"; there's no "e" on the end of it and I'm a vicar.'

'But you said.......' she began.

'Oh, for goodness' sake, just put c/o The Vicarage! I'll be back in two hours. Please have it ready by then.'

He rushed out of the door, just in time to see a Traffic Warden stepping back to admire his handiwork, having put a parking ticket under the windscreen wiper of his car. I know he had every justification for being annoyed, but I never thought the day would come when I'd hear a vicar using that sort of language. I was somewhat surprised at the extent of his vocabulary. Having collected my jacket, I went back to the office, wondering what Mr. Clarke would have thought of the furore his choice of house name had caused.

I sat down at my desk and was about to pick up my diary, when the telephone rang. Cindy told me it was my neighbour, the doctor, and she put him through.

'Great news!' he exclaimed excitedly. 'This problem you and your friend have got; it's MAD!'

'Well, I wouldn't put it quite as strongly as that,' I said. 'Certainly some of the interpretations of the Property Misdescriptions Act have been a bit daft, but.......'

'No, no,' he interrupted. 'Not mad - M....A....D....' he spelt out. 'It's an acronym: Misleading Adjectives Deficiency. Estate agents and developers throughout the U.K. are now affected, especially in the major cities.'

It transpired that he had been speaking to a colleague over the telephone the previous evening and had casually mentioned our problems. The colleague was a psychiatrist practising in London. He was well acquainted with the phenomenon and he had passed on some advice which he felt would be useful to sufferers.

It appeared that only estate agents and developers were affected, and the symptoms were exactly the same as the ones I had described to the doctor. He told me that he was quite happy to relay the advice to me and there would probably be no need for me to trouble my own G.P. I thanked him profusely for his help, and in a state of elation, rang Frank.

Again, he happened to answer the telephone. I interrupted the infuriating blather and told him that I had some excellent news. I arranged to meet him at our usual haunt at lunchtime two days hence when we both had time to spare.

The big day arrived and I set off for the Monarch's Arms. On the way to the car park, I happened to notice a placard outside the newsagent's, which said 'RAVING RECTOR IN ROAD RUMPUS RIDDLE.' This seemed vaguely familiar and I resolved to call in and collect a copy of the newspaper on the way back.

Everything was still in order at the Monarch's Arms; no sign of any disorder caused by militant supporters of the Cheddar Gorge.

'What's it all about, then?' Frank asked.

'According to my neighbour's colleague, it's MAD,' I told him.

'We've known that all along........,' he started grumbling.

'I'll tell you all about it in a minute,' I quickly butted in before he had a chance to get into his stride.

I bought some drinks and we sat in our usual place; all thought of food was forgotten in the excitement of the moment.

I explained how I had happened to bump into my neighbour and that he had been kind enough to contact me with information passed on by his colleague. Apparently, Misleading Adjectives Deficiency was rife in the London area and other cities throughout the U.K. and was now spreading amongst other estate agents in the country.

The Property Misdescriptions Act had forced everyone to distrust their clients, abandon all attempts to make their wares sound attractive to buyers and continually check up on their colleagues to make sure they were complying.

The strain was proving just too much for anyone to bear and the result was that people were suffering from hyper-active imagination, with comic consequences, although the sufferers did not find it amusing. The London expert had given some hope, however, and was able to suggest a course of self-treatment, which seemed to be having spectacular results.

Frank looked at me eagerly, with new hope in his eyes.

'What can we do, then?' he asked.

'It's quite simple, really,' I told him. 'It's just a matter of getting your mind back into training. I dug out my memory course, the other day; that was helpful to some extent. What you need to do, since you haven't got one, is to do some mind exercises.'

He looked at me blankly.

'How do you mean?' he asked, suspiciously.

I looked at him closely.

'Repeat the following phrase,' I said. "A magnificent Tudor cottage with a wealth of original oak beams and a superb inglenook fireplace, nestling in a sylvan setting......."

He looked aghast.

'No, I just can't do it,' he stammered. 'I won't. I can't break the law!'

I felt immensely sad that this once-proud human being had been reduced to a gibbering jelly. It was time to be cruel to be kind. I grabbed him by the shoulders and stared intently into his eyes.

'Pull yourself together, man,' I said roughly. 'Remember you're British!'

He just sat there, shaking his head. I realised that I was probably pushing him too far and tried a more reasoned approach.

'Maybe I'm trying too much too soon,' I told him in a more friendly voice. 'Try saying "A delightful family house with 4/5 bedrooms in half acre gardens, enjoying heavenly views over unspoilt countryside."

He shook his head.

'It's no good,' he mumbled. 'I just can't manage that sort of stuff any more. A house may be spacious to someone living in a bedsit, but it wouldn't be to some oil-rich sheik.

Anyway, what do you mean 4/5 bedrooms? It's either got four or it's got five!'

I could see that it was going to be a lot more difficult than I had imagined.

'Look,' I said patiently, 'the general public is not completely stupid. They realise that what we call "a spacious family house" is considered likely to be suitable for a family of four or five people. They don't expect it to be big enough to accommodate a Middle Eastern potentate, his harem of forty beautiful women and a couple of eunuchs! Neither do they expect the "large double garage" to take sixteen Cadillacs. Anyway, when did you last sell a house to an Arabian prince?'

He sat there shaking his head doubtfully.

'It's simply a question of applying a bit of common-sense,' I went on. 'Before all this P.M.A. nonsense came into being, prospective house-buyers were well aware that estate agents tried to make a property sound as attractive as possible in order to sell it. When they later became sellers themselves, they expected the same treatment to be given to their own houses.'

'The law's the law,' he said. 'Trading Standards officers have got no option but to apply it. Therefore we ignore it at our peril. Common-sense doesn't come into it.'

'Well, it's a pretty silly law, then,' I told him. 'I'm sure that even the Skinhead from Hackney Greyhound Stadium would agree with my sentiments on that subject.'

'Look,' I went on. 'Half the estate agents in the country are now suffering from MAD, and for what? Offences under the PMA. tend to be victimless crimes, Trading Standards officers and magistrates are having their time wasted, not to mention any agent caught up in the prosecution process, and no-one's better off for it! It's like something straight out of Alice in Wonderland!'

'My company's quite adamant about adhering to the rules. Elsie insists that we get it right,' he said.

'Even if it isn't logical,' I added for him. 'Look, why

don't you work through these examples I've listed for you? If the "expert" is right, you should start noticing the symptoms subsiding. Then, once sanity returns to the business, as I am sure it will, you should be back to normal.'

Frank didn't seem to be too enthusiastic, but glanced through the exercises I had prepared for him. I couldn't help thinking how sad it was that he had been reduced to this state, as he sat there with shoulders drooping, looking pathetic.

I had to leave him to it, since I had an appointment to show a prospective buyer over 9, Mafeking Terrace again. I didn't hold out much hope of selling it, but was obliged to make the effort for the sake of the elderly owner who was relying on me to get rid of it.

As I left, I could hear Frank muttering quietly in the corner: 'A delightful pied-a-terre........ a charming gentlemen's residence with enchanting panoramic views..... a bijou residence in the best part of town.......'

He was already making progress. It was now just a matter of time.

EPILOGUE

During the next few months, Trading Standards officers started interpreting the Property Misdescriptions Act in a more tolerant way. Having shown that they had teeth which they were prepared to use if the occasion should arise, they were now happy to return to more serious matters such as investigating car dealers suspected of 'clocking' vehicles and visiting licensed premises where it was thought possible that the Landlord was watering down the whisky.

That is not to say, however, that any unscrupulous estate agent was now safe from prosecution; far from it. Officials were still, rightly, ready to spring into action if any serious charges could be substantiated. Frivolous and mischievous complaints, however, were no longer tolerated and the vast majority of estate agents who ran reputable businesses carried on much the same as they had done previously, although they now took far greater care about what they said and wrote about the properties placed with them.

The MAD symptoms which had struck Frank, myself and others gradually subsided and virtually disappeared after a few months.

Frank still had a tendency to measure building plots to the nearest fraction of an inch (he was still deeply suspicious about metric measurements, reckoning that few people over the age of thirty had any idea what they meant). He also always made a point of including neighbouring properties in photographs of houses he was selling. This was intended to show the attraction, or otherwise, of the area but could equally have implied that they were included in the price; this was one of the potential ambiguities of the

Act, which appeared to have been overlooked when it was drafted.

Following many complaints from the public, including the latest one from Col. Irwin T. Budweisser Jr., the Office of Fair Trading took a keen interest in the activities of Flogitt & Quick. After exhaustive enquiries and a thorough search through their office records, the firm was the subject of a Banning Order, prohibiting either Gavin or Darryl from estate agency work in the future. Not deterred in the slightest, they bought a run-down bar in Majorca, built the trade up and sold it at a huge profit. No-good rogues, as they undoubtedly were, I had to admit that they worked hard at it.

Elsie was also to quit the business somewhat unexpectedly; one Friday morning it was announced to the staff that he had suddenly decided to go on 'gardening leave' at 5.30. the previous evening. No-one ever discovered the reason why this had happened, although rumours were naturally rife. A replacement was installed immediately, in the person of Doreen, Elsie's erstwhile P.A. It was a natural choice. She knew the administration side of the business backwards and, being female, her appointment showed to the public at large and the media that F&W were a modern and progressive company who were willing to promote women to positions of power. Another advantage to the firm was that, although they gave her an increase in salary, it was still a great deal less than Elsie's had been.

The next time I called into the Monarch's Arms with Frank, I was delighted to note that the name had reverted to the King's Arms, and that the old menu had been re-instated. It appeared that Mine Hosts had been losing custom at an alarming rate and the Brewery had insisted that everything went back to basics. I was sure that it was a wise decision.

Michelle went from strength to strength and soon became so indispensable that I opened a branch office in the next town and installed her as manager; it was not long before she was selling more properties than her competitors. Cindy continued working as my personal assistant, not wanting the responsibility of running an office.

I never did sell 9, Mafeking Terrace. Sadly, the old lady died. Three months later, the solicitors wrote and said that since I had not been successful in finding a buyer, they would have to withdraw instructions from me. They had decided that a larger multi-office firm would have better luck and they were going to list it with Yookay Property Services instead.

It was the best news I had heard all week.